THE
SKELLINGTON
KEY

I0592813

MITCHELL TIERNEY

THE SKELLINGTON KEY

MITCHELL TIERNEY

The Skellington Key

Copyright © 2018
Mitchell Tierney

Published by Ouroborus Book Services
www.ouroborusbooks.com

Cover Design by Sabrina RG Raven
www.sabrinargraven.com

CHAPTER ONE
BREAK THE SILENCE

'Loretta,' she said. 'Don't talk like that.'

'Talk like what?'

'You know what.'

Loretta pulled her face away from her mother. They had been arguing since they left the house.

'The sleeping all day. The leaving at night. We don't know where you are.'

'I always come back.'

'You did last time, but I worry there will be a time when I check your room and you won't be in there. I don't want you leaving at night anymore.'

Loretta no longer huffed and crossed her arms like a child. She was no longer one. There would have been a time when she didn't speak to her mother either. She remembered a time when it went for three weeks. Neither of them said a word to each other. Their father would eat by himself in the kitchen and leave them at the table. Neither one of them broke their silence.

'You're not old enough to do what you want.'

'What do you want me to do? I'm not a kid anymore. I do things that would make you cringe.'

Her mother shook her head and stopped at the red light.

'Loretta… don't.'

'Do you want me to tell you, Mum? I can. All the stuff I get up. I can tell you everything.'

'When did you become like this?'

'Like what, Mum?' she snapped. 'I grew up,' she added, her neck snapping back to the window. 'But you never did.'

Her mother knew the tears rolling down her cheeks were real and not the fake ones she had tried to use so many times to guilt her daughter into listening to her. Her husband knew it was teenagehood, but, that can't be the reason for everything, she told herself. She knew her daughter would grow up, and it feared her to her bones.

'I can't stand this anymore, Loretta.'

The light turned green and the car moved across the intersection.

'Pull over there and I'll get out.' She wanted to walk to school anyway, but the only way her mother could not worry during the day, was if she dropped her off. The constant texting and calling drove Loretta insane.

'No, I'm taking you all the way to the gate.'

'You're the only one that drives their kid to school still.'

'Not everyone has a car.'

'No, but not everyone has an overbearing mother who doesn't trust her only daughter either.'

'You can call me overbearing or anything you like, but I'm your mother and I'll always worry about your safety.'

Loretta felt like crossing her arms, but stopped

herself from doing it. The sun peaked through the over-manicured lawns of the suburban streets. The hedgerows looked far too perfect to be done by a human hand. She looked in her bag for her books, she had forgotten one. She arched her neck to look at the bench seat in the back of the car.

'What is it?'

'Nothing.'

'Did you forget something?'

'No. Just leave it, Mum.'

The next intersections light turned red and her mother padded the breaks and rolled to a complete stop. She tapped on the steering wheel with the bottom of her hand, nervously.

'You can't keep talking like that. You can't tell me to leave it.'

'I know you and Dad are getting a lock for my room window. I heard you talking about it.'

'You were listening?'

'You're in the next room, Mum!' she yelled. 'I hear everything. You put a lock on my window and the next time I get out I'm really not coming home.'

The light went green and the car pulled out in to traffic. A car flew through its read light, speeding and swerving. Mother heard the screeching of tires and Loretta could smell the brake pads burning as it tried to stop. The collision was the loudest noise either of them had ever heard. The front of the car rammed into the drivers' side door and pushed the car onto its side.

The airbag exploded in a cloud of dust, temporarily

making them both deaf. Loretta screamed and flayed her arms around trying desperately to grip anything as the car was pushed onto its roof. The impact was so furious that it spun around, facing the other direction. Metal scrapped against asphalt, sparks arching into the air. Glass smashed out and cut Loretta's hands and her mother along her face and arms. The airbag popped like a balloon and her mother gargled as her throat slammed against the steering wheel, breaking several bones in her neck and sending her head upward, into the ceiling.

A second car came from the left, hitting them again and sending them rolling against the first. The front hood buckled inwards and came through the glassless, windscreen frame. It broke her mother's arm, snapping the bone from its skin. The screams stopped as the car rolled again, her mother a motionless doll; her limbs flapping and falling without care. Loretta tried to reach for her, but the car spun and landed on its roof with a crashing, explosion of glass and igniting the engine. She smelled the fuel and then smelled the fire. She screamed for help. She could hear people in their cars yelling and calling out.

Time seemed to stand still, if only for a moment. Someone, somewhere was crying. Loretta breathed in and could feel something burning. Her hair was on fire. A fiery ball of metal had come through the front and landed in the backseat. She bashed it out with her hand, but she was upside down. She cried and screamed, panicking at the thought of her hair being burnt off. Her lungs hurt, and her hands felt like they were sticky. She looked down and saw they were covered in blood. She turned to her mother.

'Mum?'

Her face was bleeding and her eyes were open, but she wasn't moving.

CHAPTER TWO
THE WARD

'Do you still get nightmares?'

Loretta nodded. 'Every night.'

'Every night?'

'Yes.'

'You need to speak to me, Loretta. That's why you come here. We talk through it. It helps with the healing.'

Loretta looked up. Her eye was still bruised, and her arm was in a white wrap.

'Every night, I feel like I relive it.'

'The crash?'

'I don't remember anything before it.'

'Your Dad said your Mum was taking you to school.'

'I remember the smell of my hair burning.' Loretta said, running her fingers through her shortened hair. It was dyed black now. She didn't like it black, but it hid who she once was.

'What else do you remember?'

'I remember lying there, looking at my mum covered in blood. Her eyes were open, and I remembered thinking she was dead.'

'But she's not dead.'

Loretta's eyes turned in their sockets, upwards at the woman talking to her.

'She may as well be.'

'Loretta, your mother is getting better with every week that passes. The doctor told you that.'

'She can't speak yet.'

'No, that may be a while yet. But she's out of the woods.'

'She's still in intensive care.'

'What else do you remember?'

'I remember being upside down. My seatbelt wouldn't come undone. I remember hearing people talking and grabbing for me through the window. The fire was spreading through the car.'

'Then what?'

'I woke up here. I had a tube down my throat. Dad was crying.'

'Do you think you've progressed in the three months since it happened? You have more memories then you did before.'

Loretta looked down at her fingernails. She had painted the pinkie nails red. She blinked and looked away.

'I don't know. I guess so.'

'You guess so?' Loretta shrugged. 'I'll see you again next week, yeah? We can talk about your recovery and see what else you can recall. Okay? Is your dad coming to get you?'

'I have to call him from the front counter when I'm ready.'

'Are you going to see your mum before you go?'

Loretta stood up.

'I'll see you next week.' She walked out to the hallway. It smelled of high-grade bleach and sterile equipment.

Loretta knew her way around the hospital now. She could manoeuvre through the hallways blindfolded if she had to. Slowly, she made her way to the front section and signed out. The young boy at the desk took a second look at her and shook his head. She stared at him, but thought not to ask. Her footsteps echoed softly as she walked through the automatic doors and outside. It was cold. She stood and stared up at the pregnant, grey clouds and wished for rain.

Home was nearly an hour walk, but her father wouldn't be able to handle it if he didn't pick her up. She went back inside to the counter and took the phone off the receiver. Her fingers automatically started dialling the number and stopped. She placed it back down. Looking down the long hallway, she could see that it disappeared into the heart of the hospital. Her feet were walking almost by themselves.

The hallway leading up to the care unit was almost entirely vacant. It was dead quiet except the hiss and thump of machines. Each foot step sounded like a stomp. She weaved her way down several corridors until she got to the front desk. There was a woman behind it watching a small, portable TV. The sound was off, and she was staring at her nails. Loretta walked passed her, expecting to be asked what she was doing here, but the woman didn't say anything, nor did she look up.

Her mother's room was at the very end. She slowed her footsteps as she approached the room and looked in. The curtain was drawn across her bed, making it impossible to see her. Loretta could hear her mother's heart monitoring machine gently beeping to itself.

Loretta stepped into the room. She could see the blinds were drawn from the window, but the light coming in was soft and grey. Loretta moved around the curtain to the foot of the bed and looked at her mother. Her head had been shaved and the stitches only recently removed. Several long, fleshy, strings of scar tissue ran around her head, from her left eye, up to the crown of her head and over her left ear. One eye was taped shut while the other remained closed. Her fingers were still in a metal brace; bars going into her wrists and fingers to keep them straight. Loretta began to cry. Bandages wrapped her right arm, all the way up to the elbow and a plaster was covering her right foot and shin. Bloodied bandages lay on her chest and throat.

'Mum,' she said.

There was no answer. She turned away and held her head in her hands. She left the ward without saying another word.

CHAPTER THREE
THE BONE CAGE

Loretta's father sat and stared at his spaghetti and meat balls. He twisted the pasta around on his fork and brought it up to his mouth. His lips parted, but he was no longer hungry. He hadn't been hungry since the accident. He put the fork back down and pushed the bowl away. Loretta looked at him.

'Dad.'

For a moment she thought he hadn't heard her. He finally looked up as she was about to say it again.

'Are you okay, Loretta?' he said, a worried look on his face. His eyes brows were bunched together.

'Did you see Mum today?'

He nodded. 'I went before work.'

'Any improvement?'

He shook his head and looked at the empty space in front of him.

'Not yet. The doctors say she should wake up soon. Her brain activity is spiking. They think it will…' he stopped half way through his sentence and took a deep breath, 'they think it will ignite something in her brain to wake her up.'

'They said she may never speak again.'

He looked away, towards the dining room

window. The curtains were pulled across. He stood up and tucked his chair in, then went to walk away. He turned and came back to the table and sat back down.

'Sorry, I forgot you hadn't finished eating.'

'It's okay, Dad. You can go. I'll finish in my room.'

He remained seated.

'The doctors say a lot of things. No one is really sure. She may walk again, she may speak again, and it could be any day now… no one knows for sure.'

Loretta nodded. She picked up a meatball and noticed she had lost her appetite as well.

'You go to bed, I'll clean the kitchen.'

'Are you sure?'

'Yeah, it's just packing the dishwasher. I'll turn it on and you can unpack it tomorrow. I've got to study anyway.'

Her father nodded and left the table. Loretta waited and listened for his footsteps up the staircase and along the wooden floor to his room. She heard the door shut. The room was quiet and still. She emptied her plate in the bin and packed the dishes like she said she would. Checking the front door and all the windows, she then turned the lights off and made her way to her room and shut the door behind her.

Loretta hadn't actually been back to school since she left the hospital and came home after the accident. Her father was barely home, he was either at work or at the hospital. He was grateful that she was home when he got home and never, ever asked about school or where she had been during the day.

She checked her social media, but found the contents lacklustre and uninteresting. It was hard to see the smiling faces and photos of great food and the beach when she had been through a horrific accident. Having fun, or seeing others having fun just made her mad. She shut her laptop and climbed into bed. The room light remained on and it had been that way for months. Not since she was a small girl had she left the lights on. It wasn't because of imaginary monsters, or moving shadows, it was letting the night know she was still awake.

She dreamt of the old car. In her dreams she was little, far younger than she was now. She was in the backseat and her parents were in the front. They were arguing. She remembers them arguing a lot when she was younger. As she grew, the bickering lessened, or they just got better at hiding it. The car moved forward into traffic and suddenly she was in the front seat. She turned to her mother, but she was gone. She was staring at herself driving. Cars came from each direction, as fast as they could drive. She started to scream out, her hands went to her ears and she braced for impact.

The silence of the house was broken by the phone ringing. Loretta sat bolt upright. She looked at her phone, it was after 2 a.m. She heard her father move about the house, so she got up as well. She went to the hallway. Her father walked past her without saying a word. He reached for the phone in the hallway.

'Yes, hello?' Loretta could hear scrambled voices.

'Yes, this is Henry Davis. Okay, yes, I'll be straight up.'

He hung up the phone and looked at his daughter, who looked equally distraught. He had tears rolling down his face.

'Your mother has woken up.'

They barely got dressed; only throwing on robes and a pair of shoes with no socks and ran down to the car. Her father was so scared his hands were shaking. He clicked the button to open the automatic door as Loretta slid into the passenger seat and put her seatbelt on. She had barely been in cars since the accident and every time she did, it made her heart beat a little faster. She put her hand on her father's hand to steady him.

'It's okay, Dad. It's going to be okay,' she told him.

He took a deep breath and looked at her. She could see he was scared.

There was no traffic on the road, and they got to the hospital far quicker than normal. Loretta noticed an abundance of ambulances around the emergency wing. She rushed to follow her father who was heading towards the elevator.

'What if she's…' he started.

'Not the same?' Loretta finished for him. 'Don't worry, Dad. She's awake, that's the main thing.'

They sprinted down the hallway, Loretta already in tears. They made it to her bedroom and ran in, both of them struggling for breath. A doctor was beside their mother, her hand in hers. She was taking her pulse. She looked startled as the two rushed in.

Her mother had one eye open. The other was still taped shut. Her stare moved from the window to her daughter and instantly filled with tears. Loretta ran to her and could only feel one of her mother's hands on her back, it had no strength at all. Her father hugged her and kissed her. He wiped away tears and sat on the chair beside the bed, pulling it as close to the bed as he could.

'How are you feeling? I can't believe you're awake.'

'She can't speak still,' the doctor explained. 'The bone cage around her vocal chords was damaged. It will take some time to get her full voice back. She should be able to whisper in a few days.'

'Oh, thank you, thank you.'

'It's your wife Mr Davis. I've not seen many people pull through and wake up from this many injuries. She's a very tough woman.'

'Can she come home?' Loretta asked, sitting on the foot of the bed.

'Not yet, I'm afraid. She still needs regular bandage swaps and monitoring. My estimate would be a week at the very earliest.'

Loretta looked at her father, they both smiled.

'Now, I'll let you be with her for a few minutes longer, then she has to get some sleep. You can come back tomorrow in the normal visiting hours.' The doctor jotted down the vitals on the clipboard and left the room.

They held hands and wept, staring at each other in bewilderment. She tried to communicate, but her body was too weak. They stayed and spoke to her, holding her hand and telling her how worried they had been. Loretta wanted to say more, say something to her, but she couldn't find the words.

They stayed longer then allowed and then finally left when she fell asleep. They got home at day break.

CHAPTER FOUR
THE REQUEST

Henry was still in his work clothes. He had finished early and went straight to the hospital. His tie was undone slightly and hanging crooked to one side. He opened a large carry bag and started putting all his wife's gifts and spare clothes in it. He wasn't concerned with folding anything, or putting it in neatly, he was excited to take her home.

Lilith sat on the bed. Her arm had recently healed enough for the doctors to take out the metal plates and screws. It was swollen and still purple. He placed soft slippers on her feet and looked up to her and smiled. She tried to speak. Henry put his ear to her lips.

'I can't wear those... around here,' she struggled to say. 'Embarrassing.'

Henry laughed. 'It's a hospital. I saw a lady coming in here that wasn't wearing anything on her feet. Plus, it's only to the car. Hopefully we won't be back here any time soon.'

He helped her to her feet, but she became wobbly and unsteady. She started to fall back when Henry caught her and lay her back down on the bed.

'Are you sure you're ready to come home? I mean... I know the doctor said so, but...'

She nodded her assurance. She stayed seated until the nurse came by and gave her the discharge papers.

'She'll be unwell and sore for a few weeks. If there's any problems, come straight back to the emergency ward, okay?'

'Yes,' Henry nodded, staring at his wife with a worried look on his face.

The nurse left and came back with a wheelchair and took her out to the car. He helped her in to the passenger seat and did her seatbelt up. He drove slowly home, avoiding the area where the accident had occurred.

Once inside the house, Lilith motioned towards the couch with her hand.

'You really should be in bed,' Henry advised.

She tried to talk, but her throat only softly gasped. He lay her down and went upstairs. Loretta's bedroom door was shut, and he gently knocked on it. There was no answer, so he opened it. The bed hadn't been made from the night before and the window was half opened.

'Loretta?' he asked the empty room. He sighed and re-shut the door.

Henry lay with his wife on the couch through the evening and into the night. Lilith slept and when she was in too much pain she moaned softly. Henry would fetch her medication and give it to her with water. He wasn't sure why the hospital let her go home, but he was glad she was. They slept, with her curled up into him. During the night Lilith had woken and was startled.

'It's okay,' he said. 'You're home. You're not at the hospital anymore.' Her eyes glazed over and rolled back into her head. 'Lilith!' Henry held her, and she began to speak.

'You need to take me to my family home,' she said, her words so soft he could barely make it out. 'The Skellington manor. Take me there. I will rest and heal there… not here.'

Henry had his ear pushed against her lips.

'Your family home?' He pulled away, perplexed. She nodded. 'But you said no one's lived there for nearly a hundred years?'

Her fragile hand went up to his face and gently caressed it. She blinked and began to drift back into sleep.

Henry lay her head on the pillow and pulled the blanket up to her chin. He stood there looking at her bruised and broken body. If that's where she needed to recuperate, then that is what he would do. He thought about getting away from work and spending his time caring for his wife. He had made the decision right then and there, that they would go to the Manor.

There was the sound of light footsteps upstairs and Henry looked up. He went up the stairs and moved along the hallway to Loretta's' room.

'Loretta?'

'Dad?'

The door was opened an inch. Loretta looked dressed. She had shoes on and a backpack.

'Where have you been?'

'What? Nowhere. I've been here.'

'Your mother's home.'

'She is? Was that today? So much study, I thought it was tomorrow…'

There was a silence were both of them knew she was lying.

'She's on the couch downstairs, asleep. I need to talk to you.'

'Dad, can it wait till tomorrow? I gotta go to bed. There's a test tomorrow.'

'I know you haven't been to school.'

Another awkward silence followed.

'What are you talking about? Of course, I have.'

'We'll talk tomorrow, yeah? Okay.'

The door shut hard.

CHAPTER FIVE
MARSDEN WILLOW

Lilith sat the table. Her hand was still purple and yellow with bruising. Her left eye was open now, but barely. Both eyelids were engorged with scar tissue, and the muscles bloated. There was a plate of food in front of her, but she hadn't eaten any of it. She was able to pick up her fork and push it into the spaghetti, but she had lost all her strength. The teeth she did have left ached and throbbed in her mouth. She didn't say anything. Loretta looked at her mother. She didn't feel like spaghetti again, but it was really all her father could make. When her mother was in the hospital, they ordered pizza or burgers and more often than not, sat in silence and stared at their meals in a quiet house.

'We have something to run past you, Loretta,' her father said finally.

Her head snapped around to him. He had been so quiet she hardly knew he was in the room.

'What?'

'Your mother wants to go to her family home to rest and heal. It's a long way from here and we'll be gone for some time.'

Loretta looked at her mother, then back to her

father. 'Okay. How long?'

'At a guess... two to three months.'

Loretta had a blank look on her face, then she nodded. 'What family home?'

Henry looked at his wife, but her eyes were closed, trying to ignore the pain in her arm and legs.

'We've never really talked about it much, if at all. It's out in the country, miles from anywhere in a place called Marsden Willow.'

'Marsden Willow?' Loretta repeated, the name sounding somewhat familiar.

'Your mother's family have been in and around this area for a very long time. She's ninth generation. Her parents and grandparents were all there until their passing. You never got to meet them, and I only met her parents once. That one time was to ask her father for his daughter's hand in marriage.'

'So, you want to go to this old house in the middle of nowhere, apparently surrounded by nothing, so Mum can get better? Why not here, near the hospital?' She looked at her mother again.

'Your mother,' he started, looking concerned, 'has had enough of hospitals. We can get all her medication and come back for regular check-ups, but this is her wish and we are going to the Skellington Manor in two days' time.'

'Alright,' Loretta said, a little stunned. 'I'll look after the house and when you come in for check-ups, I'll see you then and hopefully your phones work out there, I'll call every day...'

'You're coming with us.'

Loretta shook her head. 'No, I'm not going with you. I have school and my friends are here.'

'You are coming with us, Loretta. We discussed this last night. I'll call the school if you want... and organise home schooling.'

She wanted to call her dad's bluff, but he looked serious.

'I can't go. I'm not going to the woods in some century old house with cobwebs and no internet access... I'm not doing it!' She stood up from the table, her chair flying backwards.

There was a fleshy thump. 'You *are* coming.' Both their heads turned. Her mother was staring at her through bloodshot eyes. She had smashed her injured hand on the table, with a fist.

Loretta sat back down.

'We leave on Tuesday. Have your things packed.'

Loretta slammed her bedroom door shut and sat at her desk. Her room was a complete mess. After the accident, she couldn't concentrate on anything any longer than a few minutes. She had gotta mad and frustrated and trashed her room. She sat in the discord and contemplated the move. After tonight's episode, surely her mother would be healed in less than a few months? She did hit the table and speak loud enough for everyone to hear her. Loretta went to her cupboard and got her luggage out. She threw it on the bed and unzipped it. A mothball rolled around in the bottom. She started throwing in clothes off the ground. She tossed in shoes and a few belts, followed by several black hoodies and her army boots. She zipped it up and climbed onto her bed and sat on it.

She knew it meant a long drive. One where they may not be able to pull over if she began to feel anxious. She jumped off her bag and yanked it to the floor. The wheels squeaked and whined. She rolled it out to the hallway and stumbled it down to the front door. Her father appeared with washing-up gloves on, a plate in one hand covered in bubbles and a dish cloth in the other. He had a look of utter shock on his face.

'You've changed your mind?'

'Under one condition.'

Her father looked behind him for her mother, but she had gone to bed.

'What is it?'

'We go on Wednesday. I have something I need to do.'

He nodded slowly. 'Okay. If that's what you need. Okay, Loretta.'

Loretta marched up stairs and slammed her door again.

On Tuesday night, her parent's luggage was by the front door, next to hers. It had sat there, untouched since she dropped it there days before. Her father had cleaned the house and they ate everything they had in the fridge that wouldn't last the few months they would be away. Their house no longer felt like their home. Loretta was starting to feel a disconnect, even more so now.

She had waited until she heard her father go to bed and listened to music through her headphones till she thought they were both asleep. She then climbed out her window and along the terracotta roof tiles. In order to get to the ground, she had to sneak past her parents' window. They always had their curtain closed, but she still hunkered down and crept until she reached the tree branch. It was hung over the roof, and all she had to do was step up onto it, walk along the branch and shimmy down the trunk. It was as if the tree had known, at some point in its growth, that it would be needed for this reason.

She walked along the dark street with nothing but a few light poles to guide her way. She wore her boots and a black hoodie, pulled up over her head. Her long hair hung down each side of her jaw. The houses were all so quiet at this time of night. Occasionally, she would wander past a house that had their TV on, blasting out into the ether. The watcher clearly had fallen asleep and that's where they would wake up when the sun rose. The roads were bare of cars and the street lights blinked and changed, regardless of drivers. Loretta walked through the night, keeping to the shadows along the long, open, asphalt streets. She passed a stray dog who looked at her oddly, and she kept going. After an hour she reached the industrialised area of her home town. The suburbs had ended some time ago and the streetlights here were further apart and less bright.

She stood in front of a large building, it was painted entirely white, and had darkened windows and a chain across the front door. She walked around the side where there was a large fence. The block of land beside it was overgrown with grass and small trees. She followed a path that led along the fence line. The block was long and took several minutes to reach the end of the path. Standing in front of it, in the dark, she could see the hole she had made. Months ago, she had cut the fence with her father's wire-cutters and snuck them back in his shed before he could notice, not that he would.

She slipped in through the hole and looked at the wrecked cars all piled up on one another. There were towers upon towers of mangled and destroyed vehicles. Between the piles of metal and glass, were small inlets of dirt, big enough for a fork-lift to drive. Loretta made her way through the cold metal graveyard. She knew the turns to take and the area to go. When she first came here, she was here till dawn, trying to find what she was looking for, now she could find it with her eyes closed. She stopped to look at a car that had been ripped in half. She had never seen it before. The entire front end, including the motor, were gone. The back tires were flat and twisted to the side. In the backseat was a baby seat. She forced herself to look away and continue down the darkened corridors.

She found what she had come to see. The car. The

family car from her accident. It was at the back of the lot. She stood in front of it and stared. All she did was stare at it, under the moon light.

I am surrounded by death.

'I know.'

There is blood here.

Loretta stepped closer to the car. The indent from where the cars hit shone like stained, cracked, glass. She placed her hand on it and closed her eyes. Flashes of memories made her body jolt and quiver.

Let me be destroyed. Do not keep me here.

'In time.'

She turned around and walked back through the wreckage yard and into the night.

CHAPTER SIX
LIGHT BULBS

They had been driving for an hour before Loretta started to feel her stomach summersault and tense up. She was staring out the window and occasionally would look at her mother, who was fast asleep. She had taken her pills before they left and fell asleep while they were finishing packing the car. She knew they had planned it that way; like Loretta, her mother no longer liked being in cars.

The surrounding environment had gone from tightly packed houses, to adobes on large blocks of land, to now vacant grassy fields and pumpkin patches. In the distance, she could see a forest that rolled over small mountains and carried on as far as the eye could see. She looked at her phone and the connection bars had dropped by half. She put it back in her backpack and tried to concentrate on not being sick.

'You okay back there?' her father asked.

'I'm fine,' Loretta lied.

'You just haven't said anything for a while.'

'I don't feel well.'

'Okay,' her father nodded. 'Up ahead is a fuel stop. We'll stop for food and a rest. How does that sound?'

She looked at him and wondered how he knew

about the fuel stop, if he had been here once over twenty years ago.

'Okay.'

The knolls of cascading grassland soon gave way to forest. It wasn't an eventual introduction to the woodland, but a sudden wall of oaks and pines. Loretta could smell it, and it cleared her mind.

They pulled into a service stop, just after the forest had started and pulled into a vacant car lot. They woke her mother up and gave her water. They left the car running while they went inside. There was a small service counter and a medium sized eatery. A few truck drivers were scattered at the make-shift diner, reading the paper and having a late breakfast. There was a tall woman behind the counter wearing an apron. She was refilling the salt shakers and she stopped and stared at Loretta as she approached.

'Can I get a bacon egg roll to go, please?'

The woman didn't reply. She lifted the salt bag and drew a line in front of her, separating herself from Loretta. She walked to the kitchen window and yelled the order to the cook. Loretta looked at the line of salt in front of her, then up to the woman.

'Why did you do that?'

'Is there anything else I can get you, love?'

Loretta tried to hand her the money, but she wouldn't take it. She motioned to put it on the counter, so Loretta slid it over to her. The woman took it and did the same thing with her change.

Her father approached from behind; 'I'm getting

some pre-packed sandwiches and chips for the car. We'll do a proper shop when we get there. Everything good here?'

The woman placed the roll into a bag and slid it over to her, then stood behind the line of salt.

'Yeah, fine,' Loretta said, slowly walking away from the woman.

They ate in the car and watched as trucks pulled in to get fuel and leave quickly. The whole area was quiet, bar a few birds in the trees nearby and the screeching of truck brakes. Lilith tried to eat, but her mouth was sore, and she lay her head back on the head rest and fell sleep again.

'We'll need to get there soon and get her to bed. I don't think this driving is making her feel good.'

Loretta agreed, and they started the car and continued their journey.

After a few restless hours they pulled off onto a dirt road. On either side the trees were nearly twenty-foot-high, and the bases were covered in pine-needles and dead branches. Loretta noticed there were no other houses anywhere around, in fact, they hadn't passed a house for some time.

'It's just up ahead,' her father exclaimed.

Loretta looked through the front windscreen as they veered off the dirt road and onto another. They went through a hedgerow fence that was overgrown and left to go wild on its own accord. Above the fence, in large lettering on a wooden plaque were the words *SKELLINGTON MANOR*. Loretta thought it looked gothic and beautiful, but she would never vocalise it.

'Why have you guys never talked about this place?' she asked.

Henry looked at his wife who was just waking up. 'Your mother... well... Look!'

A deer ran out in front of the car and Henry slammed on the brakes. Loretta instantly started to shake. She watched the deer in front of them look towards the car. It stayed motionless for several seconds then ran off.

'Is everyone okay?' he asked.

'Just get me to the house, Dad. I need to get out of this car.'

They continued forward, up and down a long and winding path. Ahead of them, the manor came into view. It was bigger and grander than Loretta could have ever imagined. It looked to be three levels high and extremely wide. It had a gothic architecture that she had only seen in books and in movies, and the front door was painted black and was big enough for two people to walk through abreast. The window sills and edging that ran around the house were archaic in nature, looking as if someone had carved it from the 18th century and brought in here from Europe. Its Victorian aesthetic gave Loretta's arms goose bumps. Henry pulled the car up to the front door, scrambled out and stared up at the mansion, with his hands on his hips.

'Wow,' he said with joy. 'It's so much bigger than I remembered.'

Loretta got out and suddenly felt dwarfed by the sheer size of it. She could see the cobwebs in every corner of every window and the antique tapestry in great detail. The front garden was either dead, or overgrown with weeds, the front steps looked dilapidated and riddled with termite holes, and the top corner of the roof had a bird's nest resting on it.

'I'll go in and clear the bedroom, put new sheets on the bed and get it ready. Then I'll take her up and we can start to clean it.'

'What about food, or electricity?'

'Well, according to your grandmother's will, the electricity was to stay on for as long as it was kept in the family.'

'So, someone's been paying it?'

Her father shrugged, 'I guess so. We haven't been.' He walked up the front stairs to the door and searched his pockets for the key. 'And as for food, we'll unpack a bit and I'll go for a drive later while you stay here and look after your mother.'

Loretta followed him up to the door, barely paying much attention to his response. The door creaked open seemingly by itself. They both looked into the darkened entrance. Her father stepped in gingerly and looked around, as if careful not to upset any of the dust. Loretta was almost hesitant to enter, but she took two steps in and stopped. To the left was a massive room with couches all draped in white sheets. There was a fire place and a chandelier that had more cobwebs than the whole outside of the house had, combined. The paint on the walls had started to fade and peel onto the ground.

To the right of the entrance hall was a small drawing room. It had a horse-shoe style window seat attached to the wall that looked out of a massive window into the front and side yard. There was a table in the centre covered in thick dust and mouse droppings.

'There's a lot of work to be done here,' her dad said, near excitement in his voice.

'Yeah, a lot,' Loretta said, with disappointment in hers. 'Are you sure this place won't make mum more sick?'

'Once we give it a clean, it'll be fine. We're surrounded by trees. There's no cars or anything out here.'

Loretta stood in front of the staircase that led upstairs. She looked up and saw the balcony almost went around the entire level, it only stopped once it reached another staircase. The banisters were carved wood, delicately chiselled and mastered by a carpenter a very long time ago. She ran her fingers over the minute details; she hadn't seen anything like it before.

Her father went to the kitchen and Loretta followed. The tops were marble, old and grainy. The sink was like a horse's trough, deep and wide. There was a window that looked out into the backyard, but it was covered in dirt and dust which made it nearly impossible to see out of. Her father reached behind the fridge and turned it on. It coughed and groaned and eventually powered up the small motor.

'Well, I'm glad that works. Should we go find a room for your mother and get her into bed?'

They went upstairs. Which each step up the staircase, Loretta felt a pressure on her whole body, as if something, or someone was trying to keep her downstairs. By the time she reached the landing, it felt like she was wearing multiple layers of wet clothing. She tried to shake it off, but it remained.

'From memory… down that way is the spare rooms and this way,' he pointed left of the staircase, 'are the main rooms.'

'You were here once… so long ago and you remember where the rooms were?'

'Sort of… I don't know where everything else is. Plus, I do remember them telling me not to go upstairs.'

Loretta stopped dead in her tracks. 'Why?' She craned her head back and looked upwards.

'I don't remember why. I just did as they requested… I was trying to ask for your mother's hand in marriage.'

Henry walked down the hallway, and even though it was still daylight outside, the hallway was nearly pitch black. He reached for a light switch, running his fingers along the peeling paint. He clicked it on and a single bulb, halfway down the long corridor, came on. It flickered for a few moments and went out.

'Remind me to get bulbs when I go to the shop.'

They made their way down the hall to the very last room. Loretta used her phone for light, as there wasn't much more it could do now it was out of range. The door creaked open slowly and sat in a small cloud of dust. There was a fireplace in the far wall, but a grate covered it. Long paintings of men and women adorning either side of it. The bed was nestled between four, very large, framed poles. The night stand was antique, and the drawer handles were silver, once polished, but now left to tarnish itself dull. There was a bathroom door beyond the bed and a large walk-in wardrobe. The entire east wall was a window. Loretta did a stroll around the room and then stood at the start of the walk-in wardrobe.

'So, we get out own bathrooms?'

'Appears that way,' her father said, pulling the sheets off the bed. He looked at his daughter confused. 'I thought you didn't want to come? By the sounds of it...'

She left the main room and went to the next room which had been assigned as her bedroom. The bed wasn't as big, and the bathroom was smaller, but there was a walk-in wardrobe, half the size of the main. Loretta ran her fingers through her hair.

There was an upside of living in a run-down mansion after all, she thought.

CHAPTER SEVEN
JARS OF MURKY WATER

New sheets were placed on the bed. The wooden floors in the main room were mopped and the dust was swept. The windows were open, and the room looked completely different. Loretta looked at the sun dropping away behind the trees. She brought her bags up after her mother was put to bed. She barely made a comment about arriving at the family home, instead, she kept pointing to the guest rooms in the other wing.

Loretta reached into her bag and pulled out her school books. They were book marked with all the readings she had to do, plus everything extra she had missed while she was away. She looked at the mass of work in front of her and sighed loudly.

'Loretta!' her father shouted.

'I'm in here,' she responded, finding it strange that you had to shout.

'It's too late to go shopping, so I'm going to make some beans on toast in the kitchen, you want some?'

It wasn't spaghetti, so she was happy about that. 'Yes!' she called back.

They sat at the large table in the dining room. There was no TV or radio. All they could hear was the heater and fridge humming through the empty house.

'Has Mum said anything to you?' she asked her

father, as she scooped beans and gravy up with her heavily buttered piece of bread.

'She said she was glad to be here.' He smiled.

Loretta looked towards the window. It was so dark outside. In the city, there were street lights and other people's houses to keep the streets lit, but here, there was nothing. They had opened the curtains as the sun was setting, but now the outside was so inky-black, Loretta thought there could be someone standing a foot outside the window, and they wouldn't even know.

'Tomorrow I'll head to the store, then go to the local medical centre and let them know we are here. I'll try get the doctors address in case we need them. You can finish unpacking and look after your mother. I shouldn't be too long, maybe a few hours.'

Loretta nodded. 'I might go see what's on the third level.'

Her father looked at her. 'Loretta. Really? I told you it was off limits.'

'They said it was off limits to you... when you visited. There's no one here now.'

'I'd still not go up there. In respect for them. It's probably an attic or something. We don't need to go up there.'

They finished eating and Loretta took the plates to the sink. The water from the faucet busted out like a sprinkler in a sluggish, brown colour. It spat and gurgled, but once the pipes were drained of stagnant dirt, the water ran crystal clear.

'You can leave them Loretta; we've had a big day. We'll do them tomorrow.'

'It's okay. I'm not tired anyway.'

'You're just avoiding studying,' her father said, waving his finger at her and giving her a cheeky smile. 'I'm going up to bed. I'll see you tomorrow.'

Loretta smiled back and started the washing up. She was elbow deep in suds when she felt the strong feeling of someone watching her. She turned around quickly expecting to see her father standing there, but the room was empty. The heater hissed and clanked off momentarily, then, with a splatter and a clonk, it came back on.

'I guess I'll have to get used to that,' she said.

'To what?'

Loretta dropped a plate into the sink. It hit the saucepan and made a ringing clang.

'Who said that?' Loretta yelped, looking around the room frantically.

She wiped her hands on a tea towel and went to each corner of the kitchen. There was no one there. She opened the pantry cupboard and looked in. It was several feet deep and full of old cans and jars of murky water and onions. She shut it and went to the door that led out the backyard. She checked it was locked. It was, with a chain pulled across it.

'Who's there?'

Loretta felt a heavy weight, like a drenched cloak suddenly come over her shoulders and head. She hunched over from its weight and held onto the wall.

She spun in a circle, trying to find the origin of it, but could see nothing.

She finished the washing up as quickly as she could and ran out of the kitchen. The front door was open. She stood in the entrance way, at the base of the staircase and looked through the door, out into the front yard. The car was parked right near the stairs still. She thought about calling out to her father, but knew he would already be asleep. She marched to the door and shut it, drawing the sliding lock across, waiting and listening. There were no footsteps, or sounds of anyone else in the house. She was certain she was alone downstairs. Moving to the right, she glanced into the drawing room, nothing. Then into the chandelier room; it too was empty. She ran up the stairs and down the hallway without looking behind her. She reached her room and shut the door and stood there, staring at the back of it. There were no sounds, not even that of the heater or refrigerator.

CHAPTER EIGHT
A PROMISE

When she woke, Loretta was facing the window. The sun was up and sending long beams across her bed and onto the floor. She blinked and momentarily forgot where she was. She sat up and looked around. The room was cold and far dustier in the luminescent light. She slipped out of her sheets and went to the bathroom to look at herself in the mirror. Her hair was frizzled and stretched outwards, like someone had been pulling at it during the night. Loretta went to her parent's room and saw her mother on the bed. She had a plate and an empty cup beside her. Her father wasn't there.

'Mum, are you okay?' she asked meekly.

Her mother didn't reply. She walked around to the other side of the bed. She was sleeping peacefully. It looked like she had been washed and had a change of clothes. Loretta went downstairs and checked the kitchen; no one there. Opening the front door, she could see the car was gone.

Hope he remembers light bulbs, Loretta thought to herself.

She showered and dressed. The water that came out of the shower head was only cold. She made a mental note to ask her father about it when he got back. She cooked toast over the open stove flame and decided to venture around the yard before her father got back and there were more chores to do.

Through the kitchen was a side door. She slid the locks off and remembered the night before when she was doing the dishes. A voice had spoken. She wasn't sure if she was hearing things or not, or could it have quite possibly been the house moving on its old foundations?

The door was stubborn and needed to be pushed and finally kicked with her boots for it to budge. It whined and protested as it eased open. The backyard wasn't a yard at all, but several large paddocks adjoined by three-foot hedgerows. There were pillars and stone statues adorning the yard. A concrete gazebo sat like an ancient temple in the far-right corner, covered in moss and vines. In the distance she could see what appeared to be a maze. The labyrinth was made from hedges and trees. There was a soft fog lying in the distance. It looked as if it separated the edge of the land from the forest.

Loretta stepped down the stone stairs onto the grass. It felt soft and wet. The blades glistened under the morning sun. She covered her eyes from the glare and looked around – where to go first?

She strolled through the overgrown grass, periodically picking up sticks and stones along the way. She found a shell, which she thought was strange and put it in her pocket. She continued to the gazebo.

The vines were hanging down like a curtain. She pushed them aside and went into the flora chamber.

There were two concrete seats, covered in mud and dirt. The flooring was circular and was met by a concrete wall that went to Loretta's hips. She could barely see through the vegetation that grew on it. It was like a cocoon. She thought it would be a good place to spend the hours studying or listening to music, and out of the house. She stepped off the pergola and looked up at the house. Someone was standing in the widow. She squinted. It was only a faint figure, standing at the far window on the second level.

'Mum?' she whispered to herself.

Her heart begun to race. Suddenly, she heard a crack and looked down. She had stepped on another shell. She looked back up quickly, but the figure was gone. She stood and stared for a moment. There was definitely something there, in white, staring at her only a second ago. She put it down to the reflection of the sun, or quite possibly her mother watching her from the window. Loretta went back across the grassy knoll and into the house. The kitchen sink was running. Straining her arms, she managed to turn it off. It must have not been turned on for some time. She couldn't help but feel confused and a little scared. Returning to the staircase, she halted suddenly, the front door was wide open.

'What is going on?' She turned around to run up the stairs and came face to face with a bulking figure.

She bumped into it and yelped in fright.

'Loretta, why are you screaming?' her father said.

'I thought you were… I thought…'

'What?'

'The tap was on,' she said, nervousness in her voice.

'That was me, I left it on. I found a fruit and vegetable market on the way home. It needs to be washed. Which reminds me, can you help bring in the groceries from the car. I just checked on your mother, she's doing fine. She still sleeping, so we'll leave her.' He gave her a smile and disappeared outside.

Loretta went to the front door and could see the car was packed with boxes and plastic bags full of food. She heaved them into the kitchen and started to fill the fridge.

'I had a shower this morning and there was no hot water.'

'Really,' her father responded, making room in the pantry. 'I had one pretty early and there was plenty. I doubt I used it all, but I'll check and make sure it's not leaking.'

'How long were you gone for?'

'Well, it's midday now, so about four or five hours?' He picked up one of the jars on the shelf and studied it.

'Midday?' Loretta said confused. 'But I only got up half an hour ago… and it was morning.'

'Morning?' her father responded, throwing the jar in the bin. 'No, can't be. You mustn't have looked at the time properly.'

Loretta slowly unpacked the groceries without saying much more. Her father had thrown all the jars in the bin and wiped down the shelves. Now they were full of canned beans, asparagus, lentils and chick peas. There were tinned pineapples and pears, protein bars and boxes of crackers and chips.

'I met a doctor at the medical centre, Dr Ruth. She said I could bring your mother to her house any time. She only lives 10 or so minutes away. She was really nice and helpful. She said she had read about the accident in the paper.'

Loretta felt tears well in her eyes. She wiped them away before her father could see them.

'Anyway, she asked to bring your mother in tomorrow for a check-up. She wants to check her medication and make sure she's getting better.'

'Okay, sure, Dad. Sounds good.'

Her father looked at her. 'I know it's a big adjustment, but it's only temporary. I promise it will get better. And before you know it, we'll be back home.'

Loretta took a bag of cashews and headed towards the stairs.

'I know, dad. I'm having fun exploring. You don't have to worry about me,' she lied.

CHAPTER NINE
THE THREE DOORS

Loretta woke gasping for air. It felt like someone was pushing down on her chest. Her hands splayed outwards, trying to push whatever it was, off her. The room was pitch black and she was alone. She caught her breath and leapt out of bed. She headed for the window and looked down into the yard. The white fog slowly crawled across the overgrown hummocks. The room was chilly, and the floorboards underfoot made her legs break out in gooseflesh. She went to her walk-in wardrobe and pulled on a black hoodie. Unbeknownst to the reason why, she went to her bedroom door and stepped out into the darkened hallway.

The whole house was dead quiet. She looked towards her parents' bedroom and saw that their door was shut. As she turned back, she noticed something at the edge of the hallway. She only saw the outline of it from the moonlight coming in the top window near the stair case. She gingerly stepped towards it. The hallway floor was colder than her bedroom. She had chills up her arms and she could feel butterflies in her stomach. She inched closer and saw it was a jar. It sat right in the middle of the hallway entrance.

She opened her mouth to speak but found she couldn't put words to how she was feeling. It was pure terror, and there were no words. Part of her mind told her to run back to her room and shut the door, another part told her to go forward. She stepped slowly, curious of the shadows either side of her and approached the jar. It was the same ones her father had thrown into the trash. She circled around it, looking for anything to indicate how it got there. Then came a sound that made her bones shiver; the sound of someone humming.

She turned towards the staircase, her eyes peeled open. There was another jar halfway down the staircase. She backed away slowly, her knees shaking and her fingers quivering. On the other side of the staircase, just before the left side hallway, was another one.

Loretta backed herself against the wall and noticed her breath was fast, making her chest jolt in and out. She shimmied along the wall towards the stairs and looked at that jar. The murky water that had been inside all of them, had gone down an inch. She looked towards the left wing and saw that the jar was nearly empty. Her gaze lifted from the jar and looked down the corridor.

She could see the three doors of the guest rooms her father had told her about. Compelled by curiosity, and immense horror, she slowly stepped towards the hall. It was so dark she could barely see the end of the corridor.

As she approached the first door, she stopped and

stared at it. It was the same as her bedroom door, but the doorknob was different; older and grander. She found her hand reaching out towards it. The metal was cold. She tried to turn it, but it was locked. She looked to the next door and found her legs moving towards it unexpectedly. She tried to open it, but it too was locked. Standing in front of the third door, she tried it also, to no avail. *All the doors were locked, but where are the keys?* she thought.

She bent over to look through the key hole, but it was so dark, all she could see was darkness staring back at her. She breathed out and found herself becoming calmer. Then, through the key hole, something moved. Two eyes stared back at her, then rushed towards the door, banging on it loudly. Loretta screamed and fell backwards, tripping over her own feet and hitting her head on the wall behind her.

She'll be awake soon.

She opened her eyes and she was in bed. She shot upright and yanked the covers off her. She ran to the hallway and could see it was now morning. She looked for the jars, but they were gone. Suddenly, she could hear the soft revving of a car engine. She ran down the stairs and out into the front where her father was just pulling away down the drive.

'Dad!' she hollered.

The car stopped. A cloud of dust kicked up from the tires. Loretta ran to the passenger side window where her mother was.

'Mum, are you okay?'

She opened her eyes and looked at her daughter, 'I'm okay, Loretta.' Her hand went up and touched her cheek. Her skin was cold.

'I did tell you we were going to the medical centre today, didn't I?' her Dad said.

'Yeah, you did,' Loretta said, completely forgetting. 'I just had this dream and...' She could see worry on her mother's face. Her father looked confused. 'Never mind. I'll tell you tonight. I just wanted to say... I'll have dinner ready. That's all.'

'Okay, Loretta. Thank you. See you when we get back.'

Loretta pulled herself away from the car as it drove down the dusty driveway. She watched as it reached the gate and turned out of view. Slowly she stepped back inside and ran her fingers through her hair. She winced at a bump on the back of her head, but ignored it and closed the door.

CHAPTER TEN
ALL KNOTTED

Loretta had decided it would be in her best interests not to investigate outside today. She knew she had seen something in the window, and after last night, she wasn't sure what was happening in this house. Certain parts of the mansion made her stomach heavy and her shoulders ache. In other parts her arms itched, and her feet were cold.

She had cleared the desk in her room and stacked up all her school work. There were several booklets to complete, with the same number of tests. Without the internet, she would have to do all the readings. She couldn't look up parts of the test and answer them that way. She had opened the first book and read through the first few chapters. The first booklet was easy enough and she was impressed she had already completed it by lunch time. She went downstairs to make something to eat and considered taking her lunch to the gazebo, but thought while she had all the learning cogs moving she should stick with it. She returned to her room and studied while she ate.

Outside, the sun glared and started to dip. A heavy wind passed through the valley and made all the trees sway and wave. She had only gone through a few shirts since she arrived but decided it would be a good excuse for a break if she found the washing machine and did a load of laundry. It would save her father doing it, and it would take nearly an hour away from studying. She gathered up all her clothes and went into her parent's bedroom and added their laundry to her pile. She had seen another doorway, just before the kitchen, under the stairs, where she thought may lead to a basement. She hadn't seen a washing machine anywhere else, so she figured it must be down there. If there wasn't one, well, she wasn't sure what she would do. Having no internet access is one thing, but hand washing clothes is where Loretta drew the line.

She fumbled the basket down the long, curved, staircase and plonked it on the floor next to the door. She gripped the handle with both hands and turned. The door slid open without creaking or disturbing any dust. The staircase went straight down. She reached for an old light switch near the door and two lights flickered to life; one on the staircase, that had a landing, then turned left, and the other was down in the basement itself. She decided to go down first and make sure there was a washing machine down there, save her lugging it laundry back up if it didn't.

The stairs were old and made of wood planks; each step groaned and sounded like it was about to splinter. She reached the bottom and was surprised at how large the area was. The floor was concrete, with metal shelves all in a line, like in a supermarket. On the far wall was a washing machine, dryer and twin sinks. There were two small clothes racks that looked rusted and dusty with cobwebs. A long, flat window was about the sinks. Loretta stared at it; the pane was frosted and must have been equal level to the ground outside. She went back up and got the laundry and the powder from the kitchen. She started to fill the machine with clothes, found the power switch after much searching, and tossed the powder in. The machine jerked and twitched as it spun the load around. It wasn't a new machine, in fact, it barely looked like a washing machine at all. It had no timer, just a dial. She would have to periodically come down here and check it.

As she turned to leave she noticed something strange. The wall behind the shelves seemed to go back further and then angle inwards. Loretta reached into her pocket for her phone and turned the light on. She moved between the second and third shelves and saw the room bottle-necked down a small corridor and angle right. As she walked towards it, she noticed the ceiling had large, wooden beams instead of metal, and there were no wires for electricity in the ceiling in this part of the basement. There were no cobwebs and hardly any dust either.

Shining the light to the right, Loretta saw an odd shaped room. The light splashed over something that made her take a step back; there was a jumble of chains hanging from the ceiling, to the floor. It looked like a butterfly's cocoon, all knotted and jumbled together with hundreds, if not thousands, of keys.

Each key was long and was hooked around a chain link by a curved piece of metal. Loretta had never seen keys this decadent and archaic in her whole life. They looked like 18th century prison keys.

She looked towards the hallway where she had come from. The instinct had developed over time from sneaking out of the house. Gingerly, she then proceeded towards the key's, extending her hand out with her fingers spread to hold a bunch of them in her palm. They were all freezing cold. She shone her torch up the chains and was astonished at the number of keys there were. They weren't just at the front, but also around the sides, at the back and some had fallen onto the floor. She picked some up and studied them. Each one was different; all had different patterns and logos. Some were slightly longer, some shorter; some had rounded teeth, some had sharp teeth. They all looked ancient and were all brown, dull silver or grey.

She slid two of them into her pocket and stepped out of the room. A strange noise emanated down the staircase. Loretta looked up at the ceiling, curious and also trying to figure out where it was coming from. She followed it back up the stairs to the main foyer and it was coming from the next level, where the bedrooms were.

Running up the stairs, her hand resting on her pocket where the keys were; she then proceeded down the hallway. It sounded like an air-horn, or a fire alarm. It rang from her parent's bedroom. She walked in warily. It was so loud she had to cover her ears.

There was a phone on the side table, where her mother had slept. It had a rotary-dialling system for the numbers, instead of a push buttons. At first, she hesitated, then she ran to it and snatched it up and held it to her ear.

'Hello?'

'Loretta, it's your father.'

'I didn't know there was a phone here.'

'Your mother only told me a few minutes ago. She remembered the number too. Anyway, I tried to call your mobile, but it went straight to message bank. We were at the clinic and her blood pressure dropped very low. She's in hospital now – '

Loretta cut him off. 'Is she going to be okay?'

'Yes. The doctors think it's a mixture of her medication doing it. They want to observe her tonight. Since it's so late and I'd have to come back early in the morning to get her, I'm going sleep on the couch in her room.'

'Okay.'

'Which means you'll be home by yourself tonight.'

Loretta stared around the room, then out the window at the hedge maze. 'That's okay. Just make sure Mum is okay.'

Her father gave her a return number for the room and she wrote it down on a notepad from the side draw.

'Are you gonna be okay in that house, alone?'

'Yeah, Dad. I'll be fine,' she tried to convince herself. 'If there's any problems, just call and I'll come right over. It's a few hours' drive, so don't hesitate, okay? Anything at all, you call.'

'Okay.'

She hung up the phone and stood in the silence of the house. Her hand went back to her pocket and she felt the keys there. She walked back out to the hallway and stared down the west wing, past the stairs, all the way to the east wing. She thought of the doors. She walked quickly, as if being chased. Standing in front of the first door she tried the first key. It didn't open. She then tried the second key but is still didn't turn the lock. She tried the second door and then the third. The keyhole was staring back at her. She considered looking through it again but decided better of it.

Thousands of keys down in the basement, she thought to herself. *Surely one fits these locks?* She returned to her room, eager to bring more keys up, but thought she better continue studying until the washing finished, then she would be free to go anywhere in the house.

CHAPTER ELEVEN
WHITE FOG

Loretta woke up with her face in her book. She was still at her desk. The side lamp was on and she had a pen in her hand. She looked around, as she had done every time she woke up, and wondered where she was. The time on her phone said it was nearly 10 pm. She had slept for hours.

She closed her book and ventured down into the kitchen. Cold air hung around the ceiling, dipping to her neck and shoulders. The fridge door was flung open and she retrieved sliced ham, tomato, lettuce and the last bun. She placed it all on the bench. She had just sliced the knife through the butter when she heard an enormous crash of glass. She jumped into the air, dropping the knife on the ground. Stumbling backwards, her back hit against the fridge. Her hands were shaking.

Her body remained still for several minutes until finally creeping out of the kitchen. It sounded like a window had been smashed. Gently stepping back into the kitchen, she grabbed a knife from the drawer. Although it wouldn't cut much more than butter, she felt slightly better for having it in her hand. She walked to the front door, it was shut. Looking left, she could see there was glass spilling out of the drawing room. She stood over a piece and looked down at it. It was curved and near it was a piece of wiry filament. She held the knife in front of her and looked into the room. It was dead still. The white sheets were still over the couches, the windows were all intact with the curtains drawn across. She looked up and saw the ceiling light had come lose and fallen onto the ground.

'Scared me to death,' she said.

'You're not dead,' returned a voice.

She jumped to the side, smashing her elbow on the door frame.

'Who's there?' she screamed, waving the knife around. She winced at the pain. 'Answer me!'

The house appeared still, as if it was taking in a breath and waiting. Loretta gripped the butter knife until her palm became sweaty. She turned on every light on the ground level that she could find. She searched the drawing room in its entirety, then the chandelier room, then the kitchen and made sure the back door was locked. She checked the mud room, the dining room and all the hallways. Besides being highly illuminated now, there was no one else there.

Loretta made a sandwich as quickly as she could and ran up the stairs to her room, slamming the door behind her. She was too anxious to eat, so she left it on her study table. She thought about getting under the sheets and going to sleep, hoping her parents would get home before she woke, but her nerves were too on edge, so she paced up and down in her room.

Thoughts of a haunted house crossed her mind several times and she tried to push those thoughts out by sitting down and reading her study, but it didn't work. It was already very dark outside, and this unsettled her even more.

'I'll call dad,' she said aloud, finally. 'He'll calm my nerves. I'll just say I'm checking in.'

She swung the door open and walked down to her parents' empty room. She went around the bed to the phone and picked it up. The dial tone was loud in her ear and she froze in absolute fear. Staring out of the window, into the darkened maze, she saw a light. The phone dropped out of her hands and onto the ground. The receiver plastic cracked. Her eyes didn't blink as she watched the small light travel through the maze, around the bends, getting to a dead end and going back the way it came.

There's someone in the yard, her inner voice said. *Go and see who it is and tell them to leave,* said another voice, from the back of her head.

Loretta watched the light become faster and more aggressive as it tried to get to the centre of the labyrinth. All of a sudden, the light jerked around, as if someone was carrying a candle and suddenly fell – then, the light went out.

Loretta ran to her room and grabbed her phone, then ran down the stairs and through the kitchen to the back door. She threw the lock back and ran out into the backyard, barefoot. The grass was wet with dew and the air was much colder outside; she could see her hurried breath. She ran across the first paddock and through the ornate fence, looking around for the start of the maze.

There was a high fence surrounding it and she followed it, keeping the fence to her right shoulder. Then, the darkness peeled back to reveal a clearance. There was a wooden sign, discrete and covered in snails that read *Skellington Maze*. Loretta stared at the dark entrance. She looked over her shoulder at the house behind her and could see her parents window. She turned back and headed into the maze.

Mud splashed up her feet and she stepped on a thorn and jumped around until she pulled it out.

'Anyone in here?' she yelped. 'I live in the house now… Are you lost?'

Only the chilly air whistling through the overgrown hedges answered back. She walked a few more feet before stopping, there was a fork in the path. Loretta looked left, then right. Something in the back of her mind told her to go left, so she did. The path forked again. She went right, then left and travelled a few more metres and then turned around and knew instantly that she was lost.

'Great,' she said to herself.

She shone her phone-torch around on the ground, hoping to see a clue or an arrow showing the way out, but there was only sticks and stones and small puddles of mud. She looked up at the moon, trying to get her bearings, but she hadn't memorised where it was when she entered. Slowly, and sheepishly, she tried to backtrack. After the third turn she entered a dead end, which she swore was not there a few minutes ago. She stood staring at the hedge wall, her phone in her hand, the light turned off, when she saw something to her right. It was coming through the shrubbery. The dancing light had returned. She froze, too afraid to move. The stars above gave little light. She was only trying to move her eyes as she watched it coming towards her, through the thicket. She wanted to scream and run, but she couldn't go anywhere. She tried to open her mouth, but her voice box was locked in terror. The light jolted from side to side and slowly headed past her. Through the bushes she could see an outline of a person. The light was housed in a lantern.

'Who are you?' Loretta spoke, her brain was too terrified to even know the words were coming out.

The figure stopped, and the light extinguished. Loretta felt her legs able to move again and she went a few metres to the left, where it had been. She reached into the maze hedge and tried to move the leaves, so she could see. There was someone staring back at her. She screamed and took a few steps backwards. The figure came forward, pushing through the maze. Its long black arms gnarled at the branches and struggled to get through. Then a leg kicked through the wall and then its left arm. Loretta turned, and ran.

The darkness took a stranglehold of her; she ran blindly and without direction. Each corner felt like she was getting deeper and deeper in the maze. Her legs gave way and she fell onto the muddy ground. She groaned and checked her knee, there was a small cut. She could hear footsteps, so she pushed her body up against the hedge and curled into a ball.

The footsteps came closer. The moon above waned and studied the cryptic puzzle below it. Loretta took a deep breath and held it. The patter of footsteps stopped, and she listened intently for any noise. She could only hear the sound of her own heartbeat. Something tugged her by her shirt and she snapped her head around to see the figure on the other side of the hedge. Its arm was through the wall and it was trying to drag her through it. She screamed and tried to tug herself away, but it was strong. She thrashed her feet about and kicked off the ground. The figure's fingers slipped off her shirt and she gathered herself to her feet and ran.

Her knee started to swell, and she hobbled around the next corner. Tears welled up in her eyes as she saw the exit. She bolted for the arch and came out at the same spot she had entered. The white fog had returned in her absence and it sat along the grassy arenas like a blanket of swirling clouds.

She sprinted as fast as she could towards the manor but stopped suddenly. There was something by the rear kitchen door. It had its back to her, but was masked, partially, by fog and shadow. She could see it there. She backed away slowly, heading towards the side of the house. The figure came out of the labyrinth and saw her and started chasing after her. Loretta could hear its footsteps behind as she ran around the house and into the dark. Her arms were pumping through the air, and she ignored the pain in her knee and feet. All she could see were wobbly, misshapen shadows of trees and more hedgerows. She reached the front of the mansion and bolted towards the front door. The thing chasing her was closer. It was as if it wasn't running at all, but floating. She ran up the stairs and placed her hand on the doorhandle, but it was locked. The figure thrust itself up the stairs and along the short balcony. Its leathery body swooped down on Loretta as she closed her eyes and waited for it to attack her.

CHAPTER TWELVE
BRUISED

'Loretta?'

She slowly opened her eyes. The sun was beaming from behind a shadowy figure standing over her.

'Dad?'

'Loretta, what are you doing out here?'

She sat up and noticed she had been slumped against the front door. Her feet were complete caked in mud and she had dried blood on her knee. She tried to stand, but her legs wobbled. She held onto the door. Behind her father, stood her mother.

'Mum, are you feeling better?'

She pointed to her throat. 'They allowed me… to… come home.' She managed to say.

Her father opened the front door and went back and helped Lilith up the front balcony stairs. She was still weak and had a hospital bracelet around her right wrist. Loretta went to give her a hug, but her mother continued walking past her and, with Henry's help, up the staircase and back into her room. Loretta followed them and went to her room where she quickly showered and changed clothes. She tried to look for the maze from her window, but the house was angled so she could only see the outside fence. She went back into the hallway and saw her father heading back down the stairs, towards the kitchen.

'Dad,' she said, trying to keep her voice down in case her mother was already asleep.

He didn't reply. Loretta ran down the stairs and caught him in the kitchen, looking in the pantry.

'Loretta, why did you pull the jars from the bins and put them back in here?'

'What?' she replied, peering over his shoulder. 'I didn't do that.'

'Well, someone did,' he said, pulling them all back out and throwing them in the bin again.

'Dad, listen, there was someone in the maze last night.'

He turned to her, a worried look on his face.

'Really?'

'Yeah, I went out there and they chased me around the front of the house.'

'Loretta…' her father's voice trailed off as he pulled stock and onions from the cupboard. 'Are you sure it wasn't just the nightmares again? You know we were concerned that you couldn't see your counsellor while you were out here… maybe I could drop you off at the bus station and you could go see her?'

'No, Dad. There was someone in the maze. I saw it through the window. I went out there and they grabbed me, look!' she pulled her shirt down off her shoulder. There were no marks.

'What am I looking at, Loretta?'

'It was…' she pulled her shirt back up.

Henry stood up and placed his armful of ingredients on the table.

'Your mother is fine by the way.'

Loretta hated to feel guilty. She was now angry at her father for talking to her that way.

'I was gonna ask, I just thought you should know someone was in our yard.'

'Stop yelling, Loretta. It was a rough night. Just drop it. I'll go check around the yard after I make this and if there are any signs of a break in, or trespassing, I'll call the police and let them know. Okay?'

Loretta backed away. She wanted to curl up and slump into a corner.

'How's Mum?' she guiltily asked.

'She's doing better, Loretta. The doctors changed some of her medication, so her blood pressure shouldn't drop anymore. Her wounds are healing well, and her voice is coming back slowly. Her ribs are still bruised, and her arm hasn't quite healed properly, but altogether, they're happy.'

Loretta smiled and sat at the bench and watched her father wipe away tears as he cut the onions. He placed a large pot on the stove and cut carrots and potatoes; tossing them in and adding the stock. He stirred and left it to boil.

'Okay, show me the maze and where this thing chased you.'

Loretta leapt to her feet and led the way out to the maze. There was a chain fence across the entrance. Loretta looked at it with confusion. It hadn't been there last night.

'You went in here? At night?'

'I saw a light, it was moving.'

'Was it the reflection of something? Maybe it was a firefly?'

'It was here, Dad. It chased me.'

'Back towards the house?'

Loretta retraced her steps around the side of the house. Her father stopped and looked at the ground.

'I can see one set of footprints... they look like yours.'

Loretta felt a tightness in her chest. She chanced a look back at the hedgerows.

'You're right, Dad. I must have dreamt it.' She added a smile to try and convince him.

He nodded and they both went back inside.

CHAPTER THIRTEEN
CICADAS

Two days passed without any strange occurrences. Loretta had studied and only spoke to her mother briefly. She had sat on the end of her bed and read her assignment to her. Her mother still couldn't speak much and only nodded. She had avoided the maze and the basement, and only stayed within the confines of her room and the kitchen. Her father drove back and forth from the store and pharmacy to top up Lilith's medication. He hadn't said much in the last few days either. He sorted through paperwork on the kitchen table and often shook his head and sighed.

Loretta sat in her room and stared out the window. She found herself glaring at the gazebo. She stood up and tucked her books under her arm. She threw her sunglasses on and headed out through the kitchen door.

'Where are you off to?' her father asked.

'I'm gonna study in the gazebo,' Loretta replied.

'Good luck. Last time I saw it, it was covered in weeds.'

'I'll clear it. It won't take long.'

'Hey, I was thinking,' her father said, taking his reading glasses off. 'I thought we should throw like, a little party or something, for your mum.'

'A party?'

'We'll clean out the chandelier room. Put fairy lights up, play music and have some wine. Try and lift your mother's spirits a bit. She's been in that room for days.'

Loretta nodded. 'Yeah, sounds good. I'll help you clean the room later...'

Henry watched his daughter leave through the rear door. He knew the party was for his wife, but it was also for his daughter.

Loretta walked through the long grass and felt it seep up, through her toes. She arched her head back and let the sun bath on her skin. She had forgotten the warmth of the sun. Bugs jumped around in front of her and she saw a giant grasshopper leap onto a tree branch and eye her curiously. She reached the pagoda and studied it with her head cocked to the right. It looked far more overgrown then when she saw it last time.

She walked up the two steps that led to the landing and kicked out the branches that had blown in. She cleaned the table of leaves and sat her books down. She could hear cicadas and noticed how they only started to sing once she was off the grass. She made a clearing to sit down and opened her books, deciding to leave her sunglasses on. It was mostly because of the bright sun coming in and, for a little bit, so her father couldn't see her close her eyes if she wanted a quick power nap. She studied for nearly an hour before heading back in for a glass of water. On her return, she noticed again that the cicadas stopped and only started once she was in the gazebo. She placed her glass on the table and stood near the steps. She listened. They were loud and in unison. She stepped off, and they stopped.

'Creepy,' she said and turned around too fast, knocking the glass of water over, onto the table.

She leapt quickly and snatched the books away before they could get drenched. The water pooled around the middle and started to drip through a hole in the centre. Loretta ducked her head under the table and could see it leaking through the bottom. She placed her books on the seat and used her hand to try and wipe the table clean.

As she pushed the last of the water off the table she noticed there were several lines engraved in the granite. She examined it closer, moving around to the other side and trying to make out what it was. She grabbed a stick from the ground and started to remove the old dirt and mud. The lines went straight, then there was an angle and finally, it made a square. To the left of the square, was an odd juxtaposition of lines. She looked closely at it; it appeared to be the maze. She ran her fingers over the square and deducted that it must be a map.

'There's the house… there's the maze… but what is that?' she whispered to herself pointing to a rhombus shaped area just past the maze. She spun her head around and looked it that direction. There were too many trees and shrubbery in the way to see that far.

'Well,' she said, 'I have deserved a break.' She looked at the map and could see there were numerous small squares within it.

She stepped out onto the lawn and the cicadas didn't say a word. She continued out of the field and down, past the labyrinth and into the rear paddocks. On either side were rows upon rows of trees, all spaced out, as if delicately planted by hand an eon ago. There were several old paths that led along the woodland border. One was laid out in cobblestones; either side had a flower bed that had long since deteriorated. All the other paths were foot trodden dirt tails, criss-crossing one another and leading nowhere.

The stone path seemed to lead where Loretta was headed, so she followed it. From this far away from the house, the birds sung a little louder. There were more of them and at one-point Loretta thought she could smell the sea. She wandered along the path, with the trees to her left and to her right. Behind her the house became smaller and smaller until it was entirely out of view.

The stone pathway began to widen out and ahead of her, Loretta could see a stone wall fence and an archway. The trees around the fence line were all dead. Their branches and twigs were curled and gnarled. The fence itself was built haphazardly; with stones placed into the concrete without care or any real regard for beauty. Loretta stopped a few feet away, so she could read the sign. It read: Cemetery of the House Skellington. Loretta's jaw dropped open. She peeked through the entrance and saw nearly a hundred tombstones. Her spine shivered, and her knees became weak. She considered walking back to the house, but the feeling passed, and then she felt strangely calm. She took a deep breath and walked under the sign.

The cemetery was dilapidated beyond words. The grave markers were all cracked and broken. Some of them had sunken into the ground and moved sideways, like crooked teeth. Others were covered in swampy peat and strangled by lianas. There were dried flowers, which had been left years, if not decades before; they had scattered in the wind, the thorns still attached to the stems. The grass was high and brown and there was a strange smell to the sepulchre; one of sweet, ripe flowers and also of upturned soil. Loretta walked slowly through the catacombs of stone hedges, looking at the pictures of the dead, and reading their names.

'Martha Skellington, born 1802, died 1832. Beloved Mother and Wife,' she read aloud. The next stone was larger and grander. The cross on top raised up several feet; 'Goodwin Sparrow, Son to Ness and Husband to Olympia. Born 1828, died 1858.'

Loretta suddenly felt uneasy. As she walked along the edge of the cemetery, careful not to step on any graves, she felt her stomach turn. It was a similar feeling to the one she was getting in the house, when she first arrived; as if some invisible force was pushing her back. She reached the very end of the acreage and stood in front of the biggest tombstone on the lot – *Gwendolyn Loretta Skellington.*

Loretta bent down and clear the leaves and branches from the ancient tomb. There was a small black and white picture of Gwendolyn attached to the tombstone. She was sitting, with her hands in her lap and looking right at the photographer. Loretta marvelled at how much the photo looked like her. The thought danced around her head that if Gwendolyn was alive today, they would look like identical twins.

'I would step over the coffin if I was you,' said a male voice.

Loretta leapt to the side, her legs instantly tingled with fear. She spun her head around to see a young boy standing near the edge of the cemetery. He wore a black coat and he had shoulder length, messy black hair. His lips were plump and nearly the colour of a red onion.

'Who are you?' Loretta said, not meaning to shout.

'I'm Casey.'

'You scared the hell out of me. What are you doing here?'

Casey stepped forward, into the graveyard, looked from left to right and stepped back again.

'I live on the farm over that way.' He thumb-pointed over his shoulder. 'So, I guess we're neighbours. Unless you're... trespassing?'

'No, I'm not trespassing,' Loretta said with scorn in

her voice. 'I'm living at the Skellington Manor for a while. I was told the nearest neighbours were far away. Too far to just wander around in each other's yards.'

Casey looked at the tombstone she had been cleaning. 'I'm back for school break. There's nothing to do, so I just walk. You don't get this sort of creepy scenery in the city.'

Loretta took a few steps towards him. Casey took one back. He was standing just outside the fence line.

'So, you're bored and decide to go to the cemetery?'

'Yeah. Looks like you did the same thing.'

Loretta wiped her dirty hands on her pants and walked over to him. He didn't step away from her this time.

'I'm Loretta. I've been at the mansion a week now.'

'I really didn't think anyone could live in that house. It's the oldest one in this county.'

'Took us two days to make it habitable, and still, not all the rooms are done.'

Casey looked up, over the cemetery, as if to look for the house.

'Do you know much about it?'

'The house? Only that my mum never mentioned it to me until recently. It's her family home. I think she grew up here.'

'There's a small lake down that hill over there, do you want to take a walk?'

Together, they walked along a well-worn path towards an abundance of trees near the bottom of the hill.

'At one stage, hundreds of years ago, this lake led out to the ocean. You would have to follow it for days or weeks, but you would get there eventually. Now, it's disconnected, but you can still smell the sea.'

Loretta took three deep breaths, as she closed her eyes, should could picture the ocean; standing on the beach.

Tree roots leading down to the small lake created an artificial staircase. They had been carved away by visitors until it became deliberate tree architecture. The water came into view. The top layer was scummy and covered in duck-weed. Mosquitos buzzed around and took flight as they approached.

'I don't like talking over the dead, so I though this place would be better.'

'Why don't you like it?'

'I think they can hear.'

'The dead?'

'You really don't know the history of this place, do you?' Casey turned to her.

'I didn't know this place existed until two weeks ago.' Loretta waved her hand in the air in protest.

'When the trials were happening in Salem, there was a mass exodus. A boat called the Dark Dawn left Salem and ended here.'

'What trials?'

'The witch trials.' Loretta stared towards the pond. All the animals had stopped moving. 'They started in the township but spread out over this county. The house you're in… was where the main witch lived.'

'How do you know this?'

'I went to school here. It was briefly mentioned in history class. Not about the witches though, I had to research that myself.'

'You did?'

'There isn't much on it, that's why I walked to the cemetery when I was in school. I wrote down all the names and looked them up in the library.'

Casey's faced looked chiselled in the soft light. His hands rested on his knees as he sat on an old log.

'So, you just come back here when you're bored?'

'Not often. My parents went out to city for the day, I didn't want to go. I find the history here fascinating.'

'Do you believe they were real witches?'

Casey nodded. 'Of course. Their blood is still here. It's still going.'

'Is this the romantic interlude, where girl meets boy and they kiss and then never see each other again?' Loretta said, sarcastically.

Casey turned his head towards her. 'I don't kiss girls, sorry. My boyfriend is back in the city. He can't reach me here other than by letter. It's pretty cute. Hopefully we do see each other again. I get good vibes from you, Loretta.'

Loretta felt almost embarrassed by what she had said. 'I better get back. If dad starts looking for me, he'll never find me.'

'I hope it's not because of what I said.'

'No, it's the whole backstory of witches that has sparked my interest.'

'It was a long time ago… and by the looks of it, they are all dead and buried now.'

'But you mentioned the blood is still going?'

'The witches' blood is diluted now, mixed in with non-witches. No one probably has the power that they used to have. I wouldn't worry.'

Loretta stood up and started the climb back up to the top of the hill. They stood close by at the top and looked out over the wavering grasslands.

'Look,' Loretta started. 'If you ever come by this way again, come to the house. I'd enjoy the company with someone other than my parents.'

'Okay,' Casey said, reaching out and taking her hand. 'I will.'

Loretta watched him saunter off into the thicket. After a while, only his long hair was visible, then he was gone. The sun had started to melt away over the mountains, and it was getting dark. She headed back to the gazebo to fetch her books.

CHAPTER FOURTEEN
THE NIGHT SHIFT

Loretta's father had been up the ladder for nearly an hour, dusting the cobwebs and dust from the chandelier.

'I can't believe how much dust is actually up here. Where does it all come from?'

Loretta was below him, holding the ladder still and shaking the spider's webs out of her hair that had fallen on her.

'Is this going to be much longer? I'm starting to look like I'm wearing a Halloween costume.'

Her father looked down and laughed.

'It goes with your black clothes.'

'Funny, Dad.'

He climbed down and stared up at the chandelier. It gleamed in places and had a dull sparkle in others. They had taken the sheets off all the furniture and were amazed by the quality and age of the couches and the chaise chair. They looked beyond antique, in fact, they looked ancient. The wood panelling was carved by hand, intricate and delicate. The stitching was done by hand also, all of it accurate and with a fine line. They were all still intact and without a tear or blemish.

'Someone really looked after this place,' Henry said, taking the sheets out of the room and down to the basement to wash.

Above her, Loretta could hear footsteps. She walked to the edge of the room so the patter was above her. She followed it as it walked past the rooms upstairs and along the hallway. She looked around for her father, but he was gone. The footsteps started to pick up pace, moving along the hallway towards the stairs that led down to where they were.

'Mum? How are you feeling?' She exited the room expecting to see her on the above landing. But there was no one there.

Her father came up from the basement carrying a broom. 'I have a job for you,' and handed it to her. 'I'm going to the junk shop to get the fairy lights and something to play music through. I shouldn't be long. By the time you sweep the floor, I'll be back.'

Loretta nodded and watched him through the window as he got in the car and drove away. She swept all the dust and dead cockroaches towards the front door. She thought about her meeting with Casey and tried to think of ways to contact him to hang out again, but she didn't get his home number, and trying to search for him on social media would be impossible with no internet.

Loretta swept the last of the dirt out the door and swept the front stairs. There were dark clouds on the horizon. The thunder was soft and tumbled through the vacant fields like a rumbling tumbleweed. She leant the broom on the side wall and went to the kitchen. Opening the fridge, she closed her eyes in elation as the cool air caressed her skin. Then she took out a box of crackers and some sliced cheese, and stood leaning on the large, wooden bench in the middle of the kitchen floor eating it with vigour. She put the crackers back in the fridge when she noticed something in the bin. She stepped over to it and saw it was the jars from the pantry again. The nape of her neck tingled. She looked around, as if to see someone standing behind her. Outside, through the front doorway, she heard a car pull up. She went out to investigate and could see her father struggling with something in his arms.

'What is that?' she said, walking down the front stairs.

'A record player!' he exclaimed. 'I found it at the junk shop. There's a bunch of old records in the boot too. Can you grab them out and bring them inside before they melt?'

Loretta popped the trunk open and saw two boxes of old records. Their sleeves were moth eaten and dog eared. Some didn't have sleeves at all, but were sitting loose, wrapped in plastic. She heaved them up and lugged them inside.

'Place looks good, Loretta. You did a good job.'

'Thanks, I think I'll have dust up my nose for the next ten years.'

'So, tonight, I'm thinking we make some cheesy-bread dip. Maybe some tacos and corn chips. We'll play some music and watch as the storm comes over.'

Loretta nodded. 'Sounds like a good plan.'

They spent the rest of the afternoon hanging the fairy lights. Once they were all up and turned on, the room looked amazing. It glowed with life and warmth. Henry plugged the record player in and made sure it worked. The speaker crackled and popped, but it was part of the charm.

Loretta slept for an hour, got dressed and headed down to the kitchen to make the food. She could hear her father upstairs, helping her mother dress and get ready. She had placed the cheese and tacos on the table when they appeared at the stairs. She felt like she hadn't seen her mother for days.

'How are you feeling, Mum?' the words came out almost forced, and she didn't know why.

'I'm… I'm…' Her mother tried to speak, but pointed to her throat.

'It still hurts to speak,' her father answered for her.

He walked her into the room and her eyes lit up. Tears rolled down her cheeks and she clasped one hand over her mouth. Henry sat her on the chaise, with her feet up and he poured her a drink. The music was soft and melodic. It gave the house an eerie soundtrack that suited its gothic appeal.

Loretta poured herself a soda and sat at the end of the chaise.

'You look good, Mum. The bruising has nearly gone, and your leg seems better.'

'Still… hurts,' she whispered, then sipped her drink.

'I don't know if Dad told you, but there's a labyrinth behind the house. You probably knew about it already, but I went in it the other night,' Loretta chose her next words carefully. 'I couldn't reach the middle, and then I got lost on the way out.'

Her mother turned her head slowly towards her. Her eyes looked green in the strangely lit room.

'Don't... go... in... there,' she said.

Loretta looked towards her father.

'It's probably too dangerous in there, Loretta. No one's looked after it for some time. Who knows what's in there.'

'It's overgrown and most of the hedges are dead or dying... but it's still...' She noticed her mother glaring at her. 'I had no plans on going back in there.'

They listened to music and Loretta served the tacos. Her father ate four in a row, getting cheese and lettuce on his shirt. She laughed. Her mother's plate sat untouched.

'Dad,' Loretta said, getting up and helping herself to another one. 'Did you know there's a cemetery behind the back field?'

She turned, and her mother was standing behind her. She almost dropped her plate.

'Loretta...' her voice was raspy. 'Stay away...'

Henry came over and placed his hands on her shoulder.

'Lilith, you must lie down...'

Lilith's hand reached out to grab Loretta, but she stepped back. Her eyes equally terrified and upset.

'I just… I went for a walk and found it… It's amazing. Your ancestors are buried there.'

'It's just, we don't like you sneaking off. You're upsetting your mother.'

'I'm not sneaking off…'

'Loretta, we can't have you wandering around too far away from the house.'

'Why? I'm doing my study, there's no one out here. No internet! What else am I supposed to do?'

There was silence for a minute before her father suddenly spoke.

'We can't trust you, Loretta. We don't know where you used to go, when we were back home. Now you're starting to do the same thing here. Please stay in the house.'

'No, I won't stay in the house!' Loretta threw her plate against the wall. It smashed into pieces, sending food against the wall and lights.

Lilith rose from her lying position, as if pulled by a puppet master above her. Her legs didn't bend, but instead she swung up and onto her feet, rushing over to Loretta and gripping her by the shoulders.

'Stop being a little bitch and listen to me,' her voice was several octaves lower than her normal voice. 'You'll do as I say. That is final.'

Her eyes blinked shut then open, and she had a different look on her face. Henry was behind her, clearly upset. Loretta pulled away from her mother's grip. She fell to the floor and Henry leant down to help her up.

'Do you want to know where I go at night?' she yelled, heading for the door. 'All those nights I snuck out and didn't come home til late... do you want to know?' Her father helped her mother off the floor, they both looked helpless and terrified. 'I got a job at the cinema complex.'

Lilith looked at Henry, tears started to roll down her face.

'The cinema complex?' Henry echoed.

Loretta stopped yelling, her shoulders slumped, and she felt a massive weight lift off her body.

'I got a job, doing the night shift, so I could go to school and pay the wreckers yard not to destroy the car.'

Henry placed Lilith back on the couch and rushed over to his daughter.

'The car? The one you were in the accident in?'

Loretta nodded, 'I sneak out and go to it and just look at it. I don't know why, but I didn't want it to be destroyed. I went to the manager and told him I would pay for it not to be crushed. So, I got the job and I pay him every week and he keeps it on his lot.'

'Loretta...' her father hugged her.

'Dad, I didn't want to tell you because I know you and Mum wouldn't understand or agree.'

'I understand, Loretta. You should have spoken to us.'

'I didn't know what to say. I don't know why I go and see it. It's weird, even for me.'

'It was a major thing to happen in your life.

Everything changed… I get it.'

She hugged him back and she looked at the wall with mince and tomato dripping down onto the floor. They both laughed.

'I'll clean it up, you take Mum to bed. She's already fallen asleep.'

CHAPTER FIFTEEN
CIRCULAR HAZE

Loretta had waited all morning, until her mother and father left for their check-ups at the medical clinic. She watched the car drive down the drive-way and rushed back to her room. She opened her notebook and tore out a blank page. She grabbed a pencil and tucked it into her pocket. She ran through the house and out the kitchen door and headed for the gazebo. It had rained during the night, making the ground soft and the air sweet. Now the grass was wet, and all the worms and bugs squirmed and kicked up from the soil.

She jumped up the stairs and over to the table where the map of the labyrinth was. She lay the piece of paper down on top of it and started to rub her pencil over the top. The smudged lead pushed over the indentations, leaving a rough mud-map of the labyrinth. She stepped off the landing and onto the grass where she stared in the direction of the hedges. She looked down at the map and could see the middle. She traced the exact route with her finger and headed towards the entrance. There was a strange heat coming off the maze. Loretta placed her hand outwards, palm up and felt it like the heat coming from an oven door.

She had memorised the first few turns and tucked the map into her pocket. The ground in the maze was soft and muddy. Her feet sunk everywhere she placed them. Gnarled branches and sticks lay across the path, blown in from the storm and washed off the hedges by the rain. She leapt over them and came to a sudden dead end. She took the map out and back tracked, making a right turn instead of a left.

She knew she was getting deeper into the maze when the sun was suddenly behind her. She reached the inner circle of hedges and ran along the left-hand side. According to the map, she had to find a small inlet, just big enough for one person to slide through, sideways. It came into view just as she thought she had circled the entire hedge wall. She slid in and made her way through the remainder of the maze until she reached an open, circular clearing. There was a concrete podium, its base was covered in scripture, unlike anything she had seen. At the base were dead roses, several of them. She thought they may be gifts for whatever god looks over the labyrinth; and she had come empty handed.

She stepped towards the podium and saw there was something nestled in the middle. There were three keys attached to a circular ring. Loretta stepped closer and stared at them intently. They were more obscure and old-world then any key she had seen in basement. She reached over, without any conscious thought, and picked them up. There was silence. She hadn't noticed any sounds before, but now, she noticed the silence. She glanced over her shoulder, feeling a strange aura coming towards her. She slipped the keys into her jean's pocket and crouched down, trying to see through the maze gaps if someone was coming. She felt it move from left to right, then forward. Whatever it was, it was coming quickly. She ran towards the exit and carefully sprinted along the wall, making sure she kept the strange energy away from her. She had backed herself into a corner and went to fetch her map from her back pocket, but it was gone. Her heart raced. The invisible spirit circled her, as if she were prey. Loretta ran blindly, every dead end, she turned around and ran the other way. She watched the sun and made sure she was heading towards it. She finally could see the archway ahead of her and bolted as fast as her legs could run. She popped out of the maze and kept running; she could feel the keys jangling in her pocket.

She finally stopped when she reached the rear stairs of the house. Mud was up her jeans, across her knees and on her backside. Her hands were filthy, and her chest was heaving in and out. She stood and looked at the labyrinth. The sparkling of the caught water on the leaves was now gone. It looked dense and thick, as if he was giving off smoke.

She washed her feet clean in the mud room; washing them in the large basin and drying them before entering the house. She pulled the keys out and examined them more closely in the light of the kitchen. Three keys – all the same size, each one with a slightly different colouring. The inscriptions on each one differing only slightly.

She went to the staircase and stopped half way up, her gaze fixed on the keys in her hand. The cloudy pressure she would sometimes get when going up to the next level had lifted. If anything, she felt lightheaded. She ran up the last few steps and turned right. The dark hallway was staring back at her. The three doors, hidden in the dark, seemed to emanate an odd sensation. The hairs on her forearms and nape of her neck stood on end.

She went to the first door and selected a random key. She slid it in the lock and turned it. It only went halfway and didn't give any more. She took it out and tried the second key. It turned all the way and clicked. She placed her hand on the doorknob and twisted it to the side. It wouldn't open. She started to pull at it, the door gave an inch and then slammed back. She jumped and took the key out.

'Loretta!' She gasped in fright and dropped the keys on the ground. It was her father's voice. She ran to the staircase. 'Come down and help with the groceries!'

Loretta started down the stairs, a little shaken. She would go back for the keys later.

CHAPTER SIXTEEN
TENTERHOOKS

'This newspaper,' Henry said, sitting at the kitchen table. 'It's mainly about farming in the area and if they should dam the river up? There isn't really much news in it at all.'

He was reading the local paper – *Marsden Willow Review*. It was ten pages long and printed on very thin, nearly see-through, paper. He folded it and pushed it towards the middle of the table.

'What do you expect, Dad? There isn't anyone out here.' She remembered Casey and gave him a glancing thought.

'I thought maybe they would get the big city papers out here. I'll have to pick them up when we go out again.'

They were eating steak from the local butchers, salad and a baked potato each. Loretta had covered hers in butter and pepper and she was avoiding the salad as much as she could. She hadn't gone back for the keys yet, as she didn't want any extra grief from her parents about going into the labyrinth again. She figured she would wait until they were asleep and then go down the east wing to fetch them.

It was so dark outside it looked like the house was

blanketed in an inky layer of oil. There were no stars. The moon was glorious and huge in the sky. It sat just through the kitchen window. Lilith was staring at it, as if it was talking to her; and she was talking back.

'How are you feeling, Mum?' Loretta asked, cutting into her steak.

She didn't reply. Henry tapped her on the arm and she very slowly pulled her gaze away from the moon.

'Loretta asked how you are,' he repeated.

She turned her face towards her daughter, even slower, and cocked her head slightly to the side.

'Better,' she said with a raspy voice.

'What do the doctors think?'

Her mother stayed staring at her.

'Well,' her father interjected. 'They said her throat bones are healing very well. But it will be some time till she gets the full use of her voice back. Her arms good and her legs are getting better. All the scar tissue will eventually get less and less, but not entirely disappear. They think she can go back to work in 6 months.'

'That's good news, isn't it, Mum?'

Her mother still stared. Her eyes wide and blinkless.

'Lilith,' Henry said, concerned. Touching her on the arm again.

Lilith suddenly stood up, knocking her chair back. She opened her mouth, as if to scream and fell to the side. She hit the floor hard, her skin smacking on the wood flooring.

'Lilith!'

Henry reached down and scoped her up off the floor. Loretta ran over, her arms reaching out for her mother.

'Mum!'

'She's okay,' Henry said, panic still in his voice. 'She probably walked around too much today.'

He carried her up the stairs and into their bedroom. Loretta followed. Henry put her on the bed and attached the blood pressure machine. He checked her pulse and her eyes, as instructed by the doctor. He picked up the phone and began dialling. Loretta sat on the other side of the bed and held her mother's hand.

'Yes, it's Henry Davis. Yes, she took a spill…' he said down the phone. 'Okay, yes. It's normal? Okay.'

He was nodding and looking from his wife to the phone.

'Mum,' Loretta whispered in her ear.

Her mother started to mouth words, but there was no sound.

'Mum, I can't hear you. Do you need to go to the hospital?'

Her father was talking with the doctor in a panicked conversation. Her mother still mouthed words that Loretta couldn't hear. They were so soft. She dug her phone out of her pocket and found the voice recorder. When her father wasn't looking she held it up to her mouth and pressed record.

'If she gets worse… yes,' Henry said, the panic starting to subside. 'Okay. Yes. I will. Bye.'

Loretta hit stop and slid her phone in her pocket. 'What did they say?'

'They said she may be dehydrated, but we can't take chances. I'm to check her blood pressure in half an hour. If it's still that low, I have to take her in.'

'Okay,' Loretta breathed a sigh of relief.

'Let her get some rest for now.'

'I'll put your dinner in the fridge if you feel like it later.' Loretta jumped off the bed and went to the door. Her father was behind her. 'Let me know if you have to go to the hospital, even if I'm asleep.'

'We will,' her father said and shut the door.

Loretta stood in the hallway and suddenly felt very alone. She felt like she was the only one in the house. She went downstairs and packed the dinner away, putting the plates in the sink till the morning, then returned to her room and locked the door. She sat on her bed and dug her phone out of her pocket. She pressed play, and could barely hear anything her mother had said. She pressed the volume button up as high as it could go and pressed play again.

'Put the keys back,' the voice said, over and over again.

Her phone fell from her hand and bounced under the bed. She sat and stared. How could her mother have known? She stood up and walked around to her door, unlocking it. Slowly, she inched the door open and stared down into the darkness. The East wing was a void of blackness, absorbing any light coming through the window. If she was going down the hallway, in the dark, she would need some light.

With phone in hand, she made her way slowly down the west wing corridor. Her footsteps echoed behind her, almost a second after her actual steps. She reached the landing where the stairs began. There was a heavy pressure from above and she dared not look up. Hesitantly, she made her way past the stairs and to the beginning of the opposite hallway. She turned her light on and dust particles swirled in it. She shone it over to the floor in front of the first door, the keys were gone.

'No,' she whispered.

Her phone-torch scanned upwards and the first door was wide open. Her heart wanted to leap out of her throat. Her ribcage pounded with utter terror. She swung around, the light bouncing off the walls and floor, looking for something that may have come out of the room. The whole house was still. Loretta gathered herself, trying not to cave into her syphoning courage and run back to her room. Instead, she stepped towards the door. Her hand reached out, fingers gently touching the cold metal of the handle, then she heard a thump and the sound of running. She spun around; it was coming from downstairs.

Loretta stood at the top of the stairs and stared down into the endless abyss of nightfall. Her right foot stepped on the first step and then she pulled it back. There were no lights on downstairs. The moon shine appeared to have evaporated altogether. One foot after the next, she tenderly began her descent to the ground floor.

Her legs shook, and her phone stammered in her hand, almost dropping it again. *What came out of that room?* she thought. By the time she reached the landing in front of the main door, her legs were jelly. It was the darkest night she had ever witnessed. The whole house was black. She could not see two feet in front of her. She tried to think if the curtains had been pulled across the windows by her father, but that thought quickly turned to dust as she heard something coming from the chandelier room.

Every instinctual nerve ending told her to run; to bolt up the stairs and scream out for her parents. Her light shimmied in front of her, and she followed it. It was only seven steps until she was standing in front of the chandelier room. The sound was loud – slushing, and gulping. It sounded like gnawing. With rattling teeth, Loretta turned her torch towards the room. The noise instantly stopped. Then came the fast pounding of footsteps again, followed by the thumping of wood. Loretta stood dead still, feeling her bladder starting to loosen. Her hand reached for the light switch on the wall. Her fingers grazing over the peeling paint and dusty panels. She fingered the switch and turned it on.

There was a woman in ragged clothes with long, manky black hair sitting squatting on the table. She had her back to her and she was making a gut-turning noise with her mouth. Loretta froze with fear. The woman slowly began to turn around. Beady, black eyes stared at her through a nest of tangled hair. Her fingernails were inches long. They were cradling a dead rat, and she was eating it. Loretta screamed. It was blood curdling; shaking the chandelier glass. The woman opened her mouth, blood dripping from her teeth and she started to scream back at her. Suddenly, she turned and leapt towards the window, smashing through it and landing on the grass outside.

Lights started turning on upstairs, followed by the pounding footsteps of her father.

'Loretta!' he screamed, seeing her at the doorway of the room. 'What is going on here?'

Loretta tried to put the words together, but her mouth and tongue wouldn't form them. She breathed in and out, trying to catch her breath.

'There… was… some… one… in here…'

Her father rushed into the room and saw the smashed window. He went to the window frame and looked out in the yard. He turned and studied the room. There was a hole in the ceiling in the corner, big enough for an animal to crawl through. On the ground were droppings and left-over food scraps.

'Are you sure it wasn't an animal?'

'It… looked… like a… woman.'

'Loretta, you need to calm down. You're hysterical. I'll go check outside.'

He went to the front door and swung it open, the blackness of the night swallowed him instantly. The feeling of being isolated and alone hit Loretta again. This time it was worse. She started to succumb to the darkness.

Her father stumbled in through the door. 'There's nothing out there. No foot prints, nothing. It might have been a bat or something. Loretta, you scared me half to death. Lucky your mother didn't wake up.'

'I saw it, Dad. It was a person, crouching on that table…'

'You go upstairs to bed, I'll tape up the window and take another look around.'

'Dad…'

'Loretta, go.'

She sheepishly turned towards the stairs and went up to her room. She locked the door and drew the curtains together, tightly. She lay on her bed with the lights on, and only fell asleep with the sun peaked over the mountains.

CHAPTER SEVENTEEN
THE DROWNING

There was a knock at the door. Loretta rolled over, ignoring it.

'Loretta,' said a voice, soft, yet impatient.

She opened one eye and looked around. The house had its own smell. Not of dust or mould, but of age and inheritance.

'Loretta,' her father said, with more volume.

She slid out of bed and threw on some long pyjama bottoms. She went to the door, it was still locked.

'Why is your door locked?' her father asked.

'Um…' Loretta said, wiping sleep from her eyes. 'Unless I was dreaming again, there was someone in the house last night. That's why my door is locked,' she said, with sarcasm dripping off every word.

'It wasn't a person, Loretta. Don't go saying that in front of your mother either. She doesn't need the extra stress on her heart.' She nodded and yawned. 'We're heading off to the clinic now. Just to renew some prescriptions. We'll be back soon.'

'Can I come?' Loretta said, without really thinking it through.

Her father was taken aback. 'Yeah, sure. If you want to. It'll be boring for you.'

'I'll look around. Change of scenery.'

Henry nodded. 'Okay, be down stairs shortly. Your mothers almost ready to go.'

Loretta shut the door and went to the bathroom. It didn't take her long to dress, when you wore nearly the same thing every day, but alternated the shirts. She grabbed her phone and sunglasses and ran down stairs. She glanced sideways at the chandelier room and could see her father had put a large wooden board up where the glass was, and nailed it to the frame. Her skin shivered at the thought of that thing in there.

She leapt into the back seat and leant forward to wrap her arms around her mother. She was motionless and unperturbed.

'You must hate all this driving back and forth,' she said, as her father locked the front door.

Her mother just shook her head. Loretta sat back. She tried to talk to her several times now, but it was always met with silence or ignorance. *Maybe she's in constant pain*, she thought. *Maybe she's upset because her life had changed so much?* But all of theirs had, not just hers.

The drive was longer then Loretta thought it was going to be. There was nothing but acres and acres of grass and wheat. It was separated by paddocks of cattle and old machinery rusting in the sun.

'What... happened to... the window?' her mother suddenly asked, half an hour in the mostly silent trip.

Her question caught both Loretta and her father off guard.

'The window? In the house?' Henry said, taking his eyes off the road to look at his wife. 'It was a...'

'Bat,' Loretta piped up.

'Yeah, a big bat. It flew into the window last night. Scared the heck out of everyone.'

Lilith looked out the window and didn't say another word for the rest of the trip.

The car pulled into a winding road that led to a small assortment of shops and an information kiosk that was boarded up. It was one road, all the way to the end of the Marsden Willow county line, then it hooked right and headed back into woodland territory. They parked, and Loretta got out and looked down the small row of shops, to the very end. She could throw a ball and by the time it stopped rolling, it would be out of town. She breathed in and tried not to let her sigh become audible.

'We're going to the clinic this way, then the pharmacy. If you want to look around, we'll meet you back here in an hour.'

'Okay,' Loretta agreed, then watched her parents slowly stroll away.

She wandered up the street and decided to start on the right-hand side and make her way down. Hopefully there was a burger place along the way, she thought. She passed a local man with a wide brimmed hat who nodded hello to her. The first shop was a handyman store. There were ladders for sale out the front, along with wheelbarrows and long, wound up lengths of rope. She stopped and stared through the window. A woman was talking to an elderly man behind the counter; they were both staring at her. She waved and moved on. There was a dress shop, with a closed sign and a shoe shop with kids inside, running around. The next shop had a strange front and Loretta had to go out onto the street to read the sign; *Marsden Willow County Library*. She looked down the street, trying to locate her parents, but they must have gone into the clinic, so she went inside. She didn't expect it to be open, or anyone in it, but there was an elderly woman pushing a trolley of books away from the counter.

'Hello, come in. Hot day, isn't it?' she said, with a heavy smile.

'You're open?'

The librarian stopped for a moment. 'Yes? Why wouldn't we be open? It's Tuesday. One of our busiest days.' Loretta looked around for anyone else. The library was bare. 'Well, *earlier,*' she said and continued pushing her trolley towards the isles of books.

'There just aren't many houses around here. I didn't think...'

'Think people still read *real* books? Not like those tablets that are out now, that hold a hundred books.'

'Yeah.'

'There's nothing like holding, and smelling, a real book.' She reached into her trolley and picked a rather large, leather-bound book and held it out to Loretta. 'Smell this one.'

'Smell it?' she queried. The librarian nodded.

Loretta leant forward and smelled the cover. 'I see what you mean.'

'See, it's grand, isn't it?' Loretta nodded. 'Was there something you were after?'

'No, not really. My parents had to come into "town" and I thought I would take a look around.'

'Oh yes,' the librarian replied. 'I haven't seen you before, so I gathered you're only here for a short time.'

'Yeah, a few more weeks maybe.'

'You don't know how long?'

She shook her head. 'Not really. I think my dad is keen to get back home, but Mum seems to want to stay longer.'

'I see... and where is it, that you are staying? If I can ask?'

'Skellington Manor,' Loretta replied, looking at her for her reaction.

'I see,' the librarian said, placing a book back on the shelf. 'Pretty far away. Nothing around but trees and grass. You must be bored out of your mind.'

'I have study to do... and exploring's been interesting.'

'I bet it has... There is an article here somewhere, from a newspaper that used to be in circulation many, many years ago, before my time, that had quite an extensive article on that house.'

'Really? I would love to read it.'

'It was from the first newspaper called the *Willow Word*, before it shut its doors and turned the printers off many years ago. It only went for so long because the train used to come through here.'

'A train?'

'Yes, before I was born. Sometimes,' she said turning around to look at her, 'with the right eyes, and the right light, you can still see the train tracks in the dirt.'

The librarian abandoned her trolley and headed towards a large, metal filing cabinet. It was painted soft orange and appeared to have been beaten along every panel. She yanked the middle draw open and started sorting through the small reference cards. Loretta followed her, looking over her shoulder.

'A lot of tragedy here in Marsden Willow. They used to call this place the county of graveyards. Do you know how the name came about?' She pulled out a card and examined it, placing it back in the assortment and continuing her search.

'No.'

'The Marsden family had brought this part of the world many hundred years ago. They divided the land up and sold most of it, making a fortune. They continued to live here through the eighteenth century.'

'They still live here now?'

'Not anymore. They had a house near the water until their son drowned one summer.'

Loretta looked at her as she spun around holding a bright yellow reference card with numbers scrawled on it.

'Oh.'

'After that, they packed everything up and moved. They couldn't bear to be around the lake or their house any longer.'

'That's awful.'

'He wasn't very old either. Now, according to this, if I can read my own hand-writing, it should be amongst the papers in storage.'

'If it's too much trouble, please don't bother. I'll probably come another time and stay longer.'

'It's no trouble, it's in the next room.' The librarian marched over to a locked door and pulled her key from her pocket and went inside.

The room was dusty and stacked high with boxes. Loretta stepped out of the way as she yanked the bottom box out and heaved it on the table. The librarian flipped the top off the box with vigour and dug her hands in and pulled out a wad of old, yellowing newspapers. She looked at the reference card and thumbed through them until she found the date. Slowly, and extremely carefully, she slid the paper out and held it in front of her.

'It's old, and brittle, but it's still mostly legible.'

'Could I get a copy of it... to read when I get home?'

'I could do this page and when you come back, I'll have the other pages ready. They are stuck together and I'm afraid I'll tear it if I try take them apart now.'

Loretta agreed and paid the librarian 25 cents for the copy. She folded it neatly and tucked it into her back pocket.

'Thank you. I look forward to coming back,' Loretta

said, heading for the door.

'Any time.'

Outside, the sun had crested the halfway mark and the heat had started to dissipate. She looked up and down the street, but couldn't see her parents. She went back to the car, and it they weren't there either. She dug her phone out and noticed it had one bar of connection. She opened a new search tab and typed; *Marsden Willow Medical Clinic*. She hit search. There came back zero results.

She looked up at the left-hand side of the street, but couldn't see anywhere that had 'medical' written on it. She began to walk down the street, looking for the clinic. Left and right, all she could see were closed stores, or ones that appeared to be void of people, and customers. She checked her phone again and the connection bar disappeared. When she reached the end, she turned around and went back. No stores anywhere on this street were a clinic. She felt the familiar tickle of panic in her stomach as she approached the car.

'Loretta,' someone said, and she turned around to see her mother standing only a few feet away.

She hadn't recognised her voice. 'I looked everywhere... I couldn't find the clinic.'

'It's down there,' her father pointed, nonchalantly.

'How did it go?'

Both her parents got in the car without answering. Her mother lay back and closed her eyes.

'Find anything interesting?' her father asked.

'Not really. Pretty quiet around here.'

'Yeah, usually there's a few more people about, but it is a quiet day. Ready for the drive home?'

Loretta nodded. The car pulled out of the main road and back along the highway. All the trees looked the same and Loretta started falling asleep in the car on the way back. She woke up just before they turned into their driveway. She could see her mother was awake in the front seat and looking around curiously.

The car pulled into the drive and up to the house. Henry parked in front of the staircase and rushed around to help Lilith out of the passenger seat. Loretta took her sunglasses off and tucked them into her pocket. She followed them inside and up the stairs. The house started to feel like home, she thought to herself. She never thought it would, but there was a sense of familiarity to it now that she liked. Her father was in front of her and held her mother. They stopped at the landing and he looked right, then took Lilith to the bedroom.

'Loretta,' he yelled back at her as she stepped off the last step. 'Why is that door open? Have you been playing that room when we told you not to?'

Loretta wasn't sure what he was talking about. She looked right, down the long hallway of the west wing. The second door was open.

CHAPTER EIGHTEEN
UNTIMELY DEATH

Loretta had been too afraid to shut the door. She had only unlocked the first door, and now the second door was wide open. She had convinced her father that she was with them the whole time, and maybe it was just the old house moving. He barely seemed to have energy to fight with this daughter anymore. She had deflected her father's interest by cooking sausages and mash potato. Henry had made his famous gravy with cooked onions and they ate, only the two of them again, at the dining room table.

'In a few days' time we have to drive home. Your mother needs to see the physiotherapist and the specialist. I couldn't book them on the same day, so we're going home for a night!'

Loretta looked less enthused then her father had expected.

'Do you not want to go home for a night? Sleep in your own bed?' He stabbed a sausage with his fork and brought it up to his mouth.

'I do,' she said, her eyes looking away from him. 'It's the car. I'd be tempted to go and see it again.'

'You can. But we don't want you paying for it not to be crushed anymore. We want you to let the car go.

We'll pay for any counselling you might need, but we need you to move on from it.'

Loretta nodded, unconvincingly. 'I feel like I need to see it one more time. It's paid up to next month anyway.'

'Okay,' her father said, swirling his knife around in the gravy. 'When we leave here, you can go back once, then no more. And not at night. No more sneaking off.'

They ate and enjoyed the storm that had finally come over. They dumped the dishes in the sink and went out the front to the large, wrap-around balcony. Her father drank scotch and they sat in the dark, on rocking chairs and watched the lightning dance across the sky. The silence between them was comfortable and they smiled and pointed as streams of lightning touched the earth, lighting up the night.

'I'm off to bed,' Henry said, standing up and stretching.

'I might stay for a bit longer,' his daughter replied and looked up at him.

'Sure, just not too late.' He kissed her on the crown of her head and disappeared inside.

Loretta sipped hot chocolate and looked outwards at the grass paddocks on either side of the drive way. The stones boarding the drive lit up like grey-washed candles every time the lightning sparked. Loretta jumped as the thunder boomed overhead. She drank the rest of her hot chocolate and stood up.

As the lightning struck again, a figure could be seen

standing far from the house, by the front gate. Loretta looked at it, thinking it was a tree at first, but she could see its eyes; they were almost yellow. She turned and went towards the door, stopping just before and glanced over her shoulder as the yard lit up again. The figure had moved. It was closer, but it was impossible to travel that distance in a few seconds.

She rushed inside, as everything went dark again. The thunder rumbled, and the lighting lit the sky up again. The figure was near the front stairs, completely shadowed in darkness, its arm reaching out towards her. Loretta slammed the door, not caring if she woke anyone up. She bolted up the stairs and into her room, avoiding looking down the west corridor. She slipped into her room and locked the door behind her. She was staring at the back of the door, half expecting it to open. Her heart pounded, and she took several deep breaths. There was no noise, no banging, no thumping, and the door didn't move.

She lay on her bed and pulled the piece of paper from her pocket. The librarian had photocopied it using the darkest tone the photocopier would allow, and even then, it was still hard to read. She crouched on her bed near the bedside lamp and began to read;

...The house, one of the oldest in Marsden County, consists of three levels. The first being the gormandize; the second being the living quarters, which is split into East and West wing and the third is the...

The words faded, followed by large, inky blots. Loretta traced her finger to the next part she could read;

...after the tragedy of the Marsden family, the Skellington's acquired the mansion from Arlo Marsden, a banker at the time, where he overlooked the loan and granted them access to the house before it went for auction. The Skellington's knew they required such a large living space and spoke to Mr Marsden in private, brokering a deal before it could go to the public...

Loretta looked up from her bed. She wondered what persuasive measures the Skellington's had used to convince the Marsden's to sell before auction. She continued;

...Martha Skellington and her husband, Royal Skellington, had travelled by ship and brought with them their first child, still in utero. There was a grand wedding at the manor not two months after the purchase. A second family, the Sparrows moved into the estate also, having children of their own, the house quickly became full. Tragedy struck the utopian scenery when...

A piece was torn from the original. Loretta flipped it over.

'What tragedy?' she said, cursing herself for not check it before she left the library.

There was more under it, so she continued reading; feeling a little dejected by the tale.

...The Sparrows had a second daughter, Olympia, who was slightly older than the three daughters of Skellingtons. They travelled by horse to school, often crossing paddocks to steal strawberries and play in the barns with the newly born calves. The three Skellington sisters; Clementine, Agnes and Lilith all exceed at schoolwork, impressing their

teachers and parents alike...

'Must be who mum is named after,' Loretta stated, trying to remember to ask her later.

...an epidemic virus came across the land in the 1830s. Its origin was tracked back to a boat from Spain. The virus spread quickly, and many deaths followed. Ness Sparrow succumbed to the flu-like virus and was driven mad with fever. She was locked up in the Skellington manor until her timely passing. Her husband, Elros Sparrow ignored all warnings from doctors and kept vigil by her side until her death; he caught the virus and died several weeks later, being buried beside his beloved wife.

'A virus?' Loretta said, suddenly feeling a little uncomfortable in the house. Even more so then before. The bottom portion was missing except one last paragraph.

...with machetes and armed with torches, the locals stormed the Skellington manor, searching for the witches that came from the sea. They surrounded the house and tried to burn it to the ground, begging for justice for the Marsden child killed in the boating accident. Rumour has it, and it can be told to you by any local worth their weight in salt, that there were four sisters left in the house; Agnes, the eldest; Olympia, the adopted sister, Clementine, the scarlet witch and Lilith, the youngest and most subdued. The tale has it that Lilith locked her three sisters in the house, cursing them for being witches and running from the house amongst the horde. It is rumoured that she perished at their hands, but others say she ran into the night, never to be seen again...

Loretta placed the piece of paper down and threw her head back onto her pillow. The words sinking deeper and deeper into her head. Three sisters locked behind three doors. She couldn't fight the cloud of sleepiness as it travelled over her body, making her bones immobile. She felt a strange connection to the house, as if she had been here before, but had forgotten everything. She blinked and stared up at the ceiling, then slipped into a deep sleep.

CHAPTER NINETEEN
TONIGHT, WE EAT

Loretta was yanked out of her slumber. She felt her whole body being pulled towards the end of the bed. She sat up in a fright, staring into the dark. There was nothing there. Her head was half way down the mattress and she could feel a stinging pressure around her foot, as if someone had gripped her leg tightly. She rubbed her foot and climbed back up onto the pillows. She illuminated her phone and it was 3.45am. She pulled the sheets back over her and closed her eyes, surrendering to sleep again.

There was a cool stream of air caressing her face. She pulled her knees up to her chest and rolled over. The surface was hard and chilly. She opened one eye and looked around at the unfamiliar environment. It wasn't uncommon for her to not know where she was for a few seconds, but this time was different. She sat up, her heart sunk down to her stomach. She was lying on the table in the gazebo in the back yard. It was still night and a heavy, frosty, fog surrounded the entire ground.

'What...what...' she started to panic.

She leapt off the table and onto her feet where the fog wrapped itself around her; she could not see the ground she stood on.

'How did I...how did I get out here?' Her voice was child-like, stammering and shaking.

She ran from the gazebo and across the lawn. The stars stared down at her, watching and lighting the way. She dared not look over to the hedge maze, she had a feeling there was someone there. Her feet stung on the hard ground, becoming wet and entangled in the fog. She tripped on something and fell to the ground. Her arms spread outwards and she hit her chin hard on a concrete garden border.

'Ouch,' she cried out, getting to her feet quickly. Her hand went to her chin and there was blood on her fingertips.

She made her way to the rear stairs and swung the kitchen door open. She shut it softly, as not to wake anyone up. How could she explain to her father that she woke up outside?

She walked softly through the kitchen, the moonlight barely providing enough radiance to guide her through the array of tables, chairs and benches. She reached the rear of the stairs and stopped suddenly, there was someone standing by the front door, with their back to her.

She tried to squint in the dark to see if it was her mother or father, but by the looks of the long hair and the torn rags for clothes, she could tell it wasn't. Her legs ran cold and she felt the return of the stabbing pain in her abdomen. Fear had gripped her body, and it was cold and tight. Whatever it was, it looked like it had been waiting for her.

She tip-toed back, never taking her eyes off the wavering figure in the blue light. She traced her steps back to the kitchen. Her thoughts were to get a knife, then call out to her father. As she turned around, she screamed. A woman was standing in the doorway to the kitchen, its purple lips peeling back baring its broken and rotten teeth.

'Come sister,' it said in a voice that resembled shattering glass. 'Tonight, we eat.'

Its hands reached out for Loretta's throat, but she was able to duck and weave out of its grasp. Its body smelt of decaying vegetation and decomposing flesh. It smelled sour and its skin looked bubbled and blistered. Loretta tried to scream, but every time she did her throat tensed up, as if someone was choking her. She ran back towards the stairs and saw the other figure blocking her way, she was hovering a foot off the ground with her arms spread wide, as if welcoming her home. The floating woman began to cackle with laughter, as if enjoying the fear she derived from Loretta. She sprinted back, avoiding the front door, as she would lose time unlocking it.

She ran into the chandelier room and towards the boarded-up window. The hammer was still on the table where her father had left it. She picked it up and tried to pry the wood panel away. She glanced at the door – they weren't there. She looked back and saw the one of them outside, staring at her through the second glass window. Its white, wrinkled hand lifted and placed its palm and spider-like fingers on the glass.

'Come to us, Loretta,' it spoke, its eyes gleaming yellow.

Loretta stepped back slowly, her teeth rattled in her jaw and she could feel her legs giving in to terror. Her gait was stammered as she stumbled and fell, she got to her feet quickly and ran from the chandelier room. She held the hammer in her hand, over hear head, ready to swipe it across the face of the other woman, but the landing was vacant.

She looked up the stairs and felt a presence of darkness, like the one she felt running from the gazebo. She ran into the drawing room and tried to unlatch the widows, but there were fastened shut. She tried to scream again, for her father, but her voice was cut off by an unknown force. She stepped back, looking directly at the large window that looked out into the front yard. She aimed the hammer, and brought it back over her head, throwing it towards the glass pane. The hammer flew, as if in slow-motion, through the air, tumbling and turning. It arced around, and its end spun over the handle, as soon as it touched the glass, it froze in mid-air. Tiny cracks appeared in the window, but it did not shatter. The hammer was touching it, and it stayed there, defying gravity.

'No,' Loretta said, staring at the uncanny sight.

'Unlocked our door, you did,' said a voice in a heavy, old English accent.

Loretta slowly turned her head to the doorway. The woman was floating a few inches off the ground. Her hair was long and matted together in flat dread-locks. Her dress was tattered and moth-eaten. Her feet were bare, and her toenails were long and yellow.

'I...I...'

'Grateful, we are. You are one of us, I can smell it.'

The other woman appeared beside her, her teeth crooked and demented, her eyes shining canary-yellow.

'Pity we need your bones.'

'Your flesh we will eat.'

They launched towards her, arms outreached. Loretta screamed again, with no sound. She slid under the table and heard them land on top of it. She ran out the other side and up the front stairs. She could hear them talking, whispering right in her ear, even though they were still in the drawing room.

Loretta reached the second level landing and every nerve told her to run to her parent's room, but deep down, a small voice told her there may be something wrong with her parents. Be it the car accident, or this strange force in this house, she wasn't sure.

She looked at the next set of stairs. They were still covered in dust and cobwebs; neither her or her father had been up to the third level. Something told her it was right. She sprinted up the steps, taking two at a time. Her stride was long and hurt her knees. She could hear the haunting figures coming up behind her.

There were only a few steps to go when she felt

their cold fingers wrap around her ankle. She was yanked to the ground. Her hands throbbing as they bounced off the staircase. She swung her head around to see one of them several metres away, her arms elongated several feet to catch her. Loretta kicked her away and rolled back onto her knees and leapt up, clutching the top step and pulling herself up to the top level. The two women screeched, flying up to the last step and suddenly halting. They stood, one of them floating in the air and the other standing beside her, as if pressed against a glass pane. Loretta breathed in and out, feeling like she was about to pass out. One of the women lunged forward, but an invisible boundary kept her on the stairs.

'You can't get up here,' Loretta said with bated breath.

'Wait for you here, we will.'

Loretta got to her feet. She stared at them, as they gnashed their teeth. Their long, congealed hair covered their faces and they stayed exactly at the edge of the last step; waiting like hungry dogs. Loretta wasn't sure what she was going to do. She looked around behind her. There was a large open area, like an attic with no door.

There were two book shelves, facing each other on each far wall. Cobwebs hung from the top book all the way down to the floor and across the ceiling to the windowsill. There was only one door, right before the right bookcase. Loretta first went to the book case. They were old reference books, mostly about the nearby cities and some were about boats and boat-building. She pretended to read one of the books, but her eyes darted over to the darkened figures at the staircase. They were still there, still staring at her. One of them was licking its own palms, while looking at her dead in the eyes.

'How am I going to get out of here?' she said quietly. She knew they had done something to her voice and she couldn't scream. Her father would have to get up at some point, she thought.

She put the book back and went to the door, the two women eyed every step she took. She tried to open it, but it was locked. Every door in this house was locked. She felt a sigh of relief knowing the door was locked, as the two things behind her emerged from the last door she opened. She went to the window and looked down at the rolling fields. She wandered if Casey's house was somewhere along the twinkling lights. She turned around and slid down the wall and sat on the floor. Her legs were straight outwards. She was tired and felt like she was covered in dust.

'All night, we have,' one of them said.

'Me too,' Loretta replied and sat and waited.

Hours passed, and Loretta found herself nodding off and jerking back awake. Every time she did it, they would still be there, still looking, still hungry. After a while, she noticed the darkness started to subside. Black gave way to dark blue.

he tilted her head back and noticed the sun was

coming up. She looked back to the stairs, one of them stepped back as the light spread across the floor. The other one waited longer, but eventually took several steps back and hissed. Loretta stood up and took several strides forward. The two women started to descend the staircase, backwards. Their hands were slashing the air, as if they were being attacked. Eventually they reached the second level, where Loretta couldn't see. She heard their soft patter of feet and a door close, then another. She waited a long time, thinking it was a trap until she decided to venture down a few steps and see if she could see them lurking in the shadows. She reached the landing, slowly and could see no signs of them. She stared at the east wing, and all the doors were shut. They must have the key, she thought. Those doors won't be locked. They'll just be waiting. She stood in the middle of the joining corridors, too scared to return to bed.

'Loretta?'

Loretta jumped about two feet in fright and snapped her head around. Her father was standing in a bathrobe in the hallway.

'You're up early?'

Loretta thought for a moment. 'I woke up and couldn't get back to bed, so I thought I would go downstairs and make some breakfast.'

Henry nodded. 'I think I might join you.'

CHAPTER TWENTY
DESCENDANT

Loretta had watched the sun go down from her bedroom window. She slept most of the day and she could hear her father calling her from downstairs. There was no way the *Marsden Word* was correct. How could it be? It was so old. No one could survive being locked in those rooms, but two of the three sisters were out. It was only a matter of time before they let the third one out, and who knew what they would be capable of. She spun on her heels and went downstairs where her father was turning over an omelette.

'I know it's more of a breakfast food, but we only really have eggs left,' he looked up at her, sweat beading on his brow. He looked worried.

'No, it's great.' Loretta scanned the room for her mother, but she wasn't there.

She sat at the table as her father brought the hot pan over, sliding the omelette onto her plate. He dropped one onto his plate and a spare one for Lilith. He dropped the pan into the washing water and it hissed and sizzled. He sat down and reached for the tomato sauce. Loretta took a mouth full of omelette and was thinking about the sisters directly above them.

'Dad,' she started.

'Yeah.'

'Ever experience anything strange happening here? Like… things in the house?'

'Like the rats and cockroaches?'

There was movement by the door and they both glanced over. Lilith was standing on the steps leading down into the kitchen.

'Mum?'

'Lilith?'

They both stood up; Loretta knocking her fork to the ground.

'I felt…better. I wanted to come and…join you for dinner,' Henry rushed over to her, but she waved him away. 'I'm okay, Hank. I'm feeling good. Let me…walk to the table on my own.'

Loretta got her a fork and set a place at the table. Lilith had trouble pulling her chair out, but she let her husband do it for her.

'You're feeling better. That's awesome, Mum.'

'I'm not…' she took a deep breath, 'entirely better. Just tonight. I felt like getting out of the… room. All I see is…hospitals and the room upstairs.'

'There's a gazebo here. You probably remember it from when you lived here as a girl.'

Lilith shook her head. 'A gazebo?'

'Yeah, it's in the yard. Maybe tomorrow we can go out there. Have lunch there.'

'Loretta,' her father piped up. 'You won't be dragging your mother around the yard…not yet.'

'It's okay. I take one day at a time.'

She picked at her omelette and started to eat. Loretta sat back down and had this overwhelming sense of family, now they were all at one table, eating together. They ate and enjoyed the company. They didn't say much, but they didn't have to.

Lilith ate nearly half and started to stand up.

'I'm not feeling great...again. I'm going to go...back to bed.' Her voice was still raspy, but had gotten better.

'Let me...'

'No, I can do it,' she protested.

She headed back towards the staircase. Henry had stood up and was watching her leave. He looked crestfallen.

'She's just testing out her independence, Dad. Don't take it any other way. She still needs you.'

He looked at his daughter and heard knowledge well advanced for her age.

'Yeah, I just ...' He sat back down and slowly began to eat again.

'So, you haven't seen like... anyone else in the house?'

'This again, Loretta?' he started to sound annoyed.

'I just need to know?'

'Why?' He looked from his plate to his daughter. 'No, I haven't seen anyone in the house. I told you, it was a bat that broke the window.'

'I may have let something out.'

Henry froze, his fork halfway up to his mouth.

'Dad?'

He didn't say anything. His fork fell to the table and the egg rolled off it and onto the floor. Loretta started at him. His eyes rolled back into their sockets and his chair started to slide backwards. His hands stayed in the same position, holding nothing.

'What's going on?' Loretta said, standing up and suddenly become very afraid.

Her father's head was yanked back by an invisible hand, his mouth wide open and his glaring white eyes staring up at the ceiling.

'Loretta Skellington,' said the voice from her father's mouth, but it wasn't his voice. It was that of an old woman. Her voice crackled and hissed. Saliva dripped down his cheek.

'Who are you?' she asked, taking one step back.

'The witch; Clementine. My name means something on the tongues in this land.'

Her father's head jolted back and forth, as if he was choking.

'What do you want from us?'

His white eyes shifted to her; he looked skeletal.

'Possibly your finger bones. But since you set us free, dear girl, I may settle just on your eyeballs.'

Loretta's skin went cold.

'You can't get to the third level… I know that for certain. I'll lock you back in your rooms.'

The witch cackled loudly.

'Our rooms? Prison cells, they are. Kept us in there a long time.'

'I read about you. You brought something

here…from wherever you are from.'

'From far away, we are. The Skellington's have an ugly past. You are one of them, yes.'

'I'm not a Skellington, I'm a Davis. I don't want anything to do with you or your sisters.'

'Loretta Skellington is your name. Ask your mother.'

'You don't know her!'

'Don't we?' More saliva dripped onto the ground.

'It's been over a hundred years… whatever you were, is now long gone. Whatever bloodline you came from has been diluted.'

'Loretta Skellington is a direct descendant. Your mother is our sister, Lilith Skellington.'

'Liar! She's only 42. If she was your sister, she would be over a hundred years old!'

'Believe what you want, girl. Your skin will look charming draped over my shoulders. Your bones will make fine runes, and your heart we will roast to nourish our organs.'

'Dad! Wake up!'

The chair slid across the floor, towards the table and stopped all of a sudden. His mouth snapped shut and his eyes rolled back. He shook his head and stared at his empty hand.

'Sorry, Loretta. I must have dosed off. I'll clean it up…'

Loretta knew then that she was on her own in this fight.

CHAPTER TWENTY-ONE
MOONSHADOW

The car was speeding forward in slow motion. Its headlights blinded everything around them and a horn blared a warning sound. The glass shattered and seemed to freeze in mid-air. They were like tiny cut diamonds on display, but soon would be dripping with blood and tearing at skin and muscle. The car jarred forward, then they were hit from behind. Her mother screamed, and then her voice went. Loretta reached for her, but was tossed upwards, then down, then to the side, hitting her head on the door, then the dashboard.

Loretta.

Her jaw throbbed and began to swell up. Blood gushed from her nose and she could see her mother's arm get caught in the steering wheel, it spun to the side and snapped the bone in half. Loretta heard it break and became sick to her stomach. The metal crumbled at the side and suddenly she could see the asphalt of the road, she could smell its heat and feel its gravity.

Loretta!

Someone yelled, and arms rushed into the car, pulling at her hair and yanking her seatbelt off. She called for them to save her mother, but could see she wasn't conscious. There came the sound of sirens and then rushed voices, screaming and angry. Tires skidded, and the car moved again. She tried to wake her mother, but her eyes were shut. There was so much blood.

'Loretta!'

She sat bolt upright and looked around the room. Her mother was standing at the edge of the bed.

'Mum?'

She was holding two pieces of paper in her hand.

'What is this?' her raspy voice croaked.

Loretta squinted her tired eyes to see. One was the photocopy from the newspaper and the other was the map to the labyrinth.

'That's...'

'Where did you get this from? And this one,' she waved the map angrily. 'After we told you not to go in there... you disobeyed us again!'

She looked to the door, trying to find her father, but he was nowhere in sight.

'No, Mum, I was just curious and...'

'Curious? Loretta, we are not here for you, we are here... for me,' she gasped for breath. 'All you've done is made it... hard on your father. He's... doing his best and you are making it difficult!'

'Wait, no, I'm not...You've been in bed the whole time. There's nothing to do here. I just go exploring... this house is amazing,' she tried to reason.

'You're a selfish little bitch, Loretta. And you've

gotten even worse since the accident.'

Her mother struggled to stand. She stared at her daughter who was lost for words. She walked out the bedroom door and slammed it shut. Loretta could hear the jingle of keys and a lock snap shut. She ran to the door and tried the handle.

'You're locking me in here?'

'You're grounded. You're not leaving your room until I… say so.'

She could hear her mother's footsteps fade away. Loretta stood face to face with the door. She couldn't believe what her mother had done. A shadow crossed under the doorway, she knew it was her father.

'I'm sorry, Loretta. Your mother is very upset.'

'I didn't do anything wrong, Dad.'

'I'm sorry.'

Then came the sound of his footsteps fading away. Loretta walked to the end of her bed and sat down. It felt like her heart had been torn out. She slumped back and tried not to cry. She felt the walls of the room restrict around her and decided she wouldn't sulk and moan, because that's what her mother would want. Instead, she got up, showered and dressed. She opened her window slightly and looked out at the morning dew sitting like a crystal blanket on the fields. She sat at her study desk and started to read where she had left off. She hadn't done much in the last few days and to prove a point, she would study and get a lot of her work done and not complain once.

Loretta studied for hours, then tried to pick the lock

with a hair pin. The lock was so old, she couldn't turn the mechanism. She returned to study and then decided to lie down as the midday sun rose high, heating the house. When she woke there was a tray at the bottom of her bed with a glass of milk, a sandwich and several cookies. She walked to the door, only to find it still locked. She tried to be brave and accept what her mother had done, but broke down at her desk, while eating her sandwich. Her mother hadn't been herself since they arrived. She thought of the witches, and knew they had something to do with it. Even her father last night at dinner, appeared to be possessed.

She pulled her desk away from the window and lent out. She was on the second story; there was no pipes or window frames to climb down. There was no hedge or garden to land on either, she looked upwards. The third level library window was above her, with what appeared to be enough exposed bricks to climb up to it. She popped her head back in just as her bedroom door opened. Her father was standing there, he had dirt on his boots and sweat around his collar.

'How are you holding up in here?' he said.

'You can't lock me in here.'

'You're grounded because you broke the house rules. You did it at home and now you're doing it here. It's just till tomorrow.'

'I can't go and explore? There's no internet here, no TV, nothing.'

'There's your study,' her father said, with a faint smile.

'I've been doing that all day. I've done two weeks' worth just today.'

'Well, you're nice and caught up then.'

'It's boring.'

'Loretta, I'm not doing this okay. Do you need anything?'

Loretta knew she had slipped into her old habits. Her bratty personality always came to the forefront.

'No, Dad. I'm good. I'll just keep studying and if I don't see you for dinner, I'll see you tomorrow.'

She forced a smile that seemed very foreign to her face. Her father paused for a moment, went to shut the door and nodded to his daughter, understanding she was putting on a brave face.

'It's your mother's rules. I would never lock you in a room. Let's just make her happy while she heals and forget this ever happened.'

Loretta nodded. 'Okay.'

By night, Loretta had packed her study up and sorted it into the "read and completed" pile and the "yet to read" pile. She was over half way and saved some of her favourite courses till last. She had sat her exams the teachers gave her and checked them, there was no way she could fail. Her father had brought in dinner, instead of inviting her down to eat with them. It was a vegetable soup, very salty, with nearly a half crust of bread, thickly buttered. She ate it by herself, in silence and left the tray and empty bowl by the door. She climbed into bed and turned the light off. She wasn't tired, but there was nothing else to do, so she thought she would try and sleep.

The thought of another nightmare about the car crash made her restless. She got up and went to the window, pushing it open all the way. She looked up the side of the house to the window above her. Then, suddenly she heard a scratching. She swung her head back in and looked around the darken room. It sounded like scratching wood. She looked towards the door.

'Dad?'

She stepped forward. The scratching was constant, like a rat trapped between the floorboards. She softly placed her ear against the door. It was coming from the other side. She leant down and could see feet. She leapt back, her hand covering her mouth.

'Who is it?' she whispered.

The scratching continued, the feet shuffling from side to side.

'Hungry, we are,' said a voice.

Loretta walked slowly backwards until her back was against the far wall. The witch was trying to get in. She was trapped. There came the sound of a key sliding into the door lock. It turned, Loretta held her breath. The mechanism stopped and clinked. The key was withdrawn, and another slid in.

They have keys, she thought. What if one of them fits the lock?

She sat on the windowsill and swung her legs

around, so they were dangling precariously over the ledge. Looking down, the ground seemed so much further away than before. She glanced over her shoulder as the doorhandle turned, but remained locked. She could see the shadow of the witch's feet pacing up and down in front of the door. Loretta gripped the window frame and stood up. The outside air was colder and made the stone-bricks slippery. Her right hand reached upwards and she gripped the next brick, pushing her body up so her foot rested on an outcropping of stone. Hand over hand, she heaved herself up towards the window. Her body shook and the breeze bit at her ankles. She tried not to look down or let the situation enter her mind.

She climbed up further, one foot gently gripping what appeared to be an old bracket for a pipe. She pushed, and her foot slipped. Her body fell, and her skin burst into gooseflesh. Instinctively, her hand gripped anything it could. Her fingertips grasped the stone wall. The rough edges ripping at the tips of her fingers. Her feet dangled and her moonshadow danced below. She brought her left leg up and found purchase on the wall, it held her weight while she caught her breath. The skin on her fingers were bleeding. Below her, she could hear a door opening. She looked up and pushed, gripping the third level window. She kicked with her legs and clambered up to the window sill.

There was a latch on the outside, which she thought was strange. She unlocked it and muscled the window open. She crawled inside, relieved. She carefully poked her head out and looked down. There were long, grey fingers resting on her windowsill below. The nails were haggard and long; twisted and covered in scratches. She could see the witch's hair as she stuck her head out her window and looked up. Loretta pulled away and hid.

'They can't get me up here,' she told herself. She reached up and pulled the window shut. There was no lock on the inside.

She waited several minutes, expecting the witch to climb the wall or float up to the window, but neither occurred. She steadied her nerves and stood up. The first thing she was drawn to, was the door. It had been locked earlier and she felt a magnetism to it. She walked over, careful not to let her footsteps echo too loud. She turned the handle and it was unlocked. The door swung open, seemingly on its own.

The room was small with a study desk against the far wall. A lamp with a lime-green shade sat to the right, dripping with cobwebs. There was a wall-shelf full of books and notepads. To the right was a map of the world, in a frame, behind glass. Someone had hand-drawn lines from Italy to Greece, then to London and then finally here, where there was a large 'X'. Loretta traced the voyage with her finger, leaving a dust-free line on the glass. She next went to the desk. The top was clear, there were a few dead flies that had somehow gotten in and couldn't escape. She pulled open the first draw and nestled amongst old newspaper clippings, was a book. She gently picked it up and opened it to the first page. *The Diary of L.S. – Not to Be Read by Anyone Else.*

Loretta carried it back to the window, so she could read it in the moonlight. She flipped through it and could see there was large sections that were hand written. Newspaper articles were glued in and folded. There were maps, a sketch of the labyrinth was near the rear of the book, as well as a hand drawn picture of the gazebo and surrounding gardens. She came across an entry and began to read;

How to Deal with Witches:

They are here, and I am one. There is no doubt about it, but I cannot sit by and idly watch as they kill men and children for their own bloodlust. After much research and experimenting, I have devised some quick and easy ways to avoid them. This is not to be used for capture, but merely to make your life easier, if they are present;

Witch's hate disorder – Spill the beans! Spill a can of beans or pins and the witch will become aggravated to the point they must pick them up. Some have a desire to count them also.

Mirrors! They hate mirrors. Unfortunately, all mirrors have been removed from this house. Show them their reflections and they will back off – petty, insecure things they are!

Daylight – they hate being out in the daylight. It does nothing to them, but the sun is too bright for their dead eyes. They can't see. A candle is too little a flame to be effective – only a bright light can blind them.

These are a few of many things I have noted in this journal. Defeating the witches, my own family, has been difficult and taxing on my mind. I feel it is of the best interest of the town and surrounding country side if they are to be locked away.

The diary entry ends. Loretta closed the book and tucked it into her rear pant waist. She looks out at the window sill; the witch is gone. She was suddenly overcome with a feeling of drowsiness. She fought to keep her eyes open, but they were as heavy as lead. She felt too weak to climb back down. So, she sat with her back against the wall and waited for the first cusp of morning light, so she could climb back down to her room.

CHAPTER TWENTY-TWO
DRIVEN AWAY

Going down the wall was harder than going up, Loretta thought. The morning brought with it a sickly, wet dew that covered everything. She slipped twice, shooting electricity up her spine in the form of sudden fear. She knew if she fell, she could be seriously hurt, although, it wouldn't be high enough to kill her. She scrambled inside her bedroom, pulled the diary from her pocket and hid it under her pillow. Her bedroom door was closed.

There was the sound of pounding footsteps.

'Loretta, quick!' she heard her father yell.

She rushed to the door and tried the handle, but it was still locked.

'Dad, it's locked!'

'Help me, Loretta!' her father's voice was stricken with horror.

Loretta pulled and yanked at the old door, but it wouldn't budge.

'Unlock the door, Dad! What is happening?'

She had an instant image of one of the witches biting at his neck and draining his blood while the other one tried to remove his intestines. She kicked at the door and suddenly heard it unlatch. She swung it open and saw her father shoot past her. He was going so quick he appeared as a blur.

'Dad,' she yelped as he ran past. 'What's going on?'

'It's your mother,' he screamed, getting to the staircase and bolting down them towards the front door.

Loretta stepped out into the hallway. On the other side of the landing, standing in the dark shadows of the east wing, were the two witches. She could see their outline and beady, glowing eyes. They stood side by side like garden statues; their hands lay flat by their sides. Loretta stepped quickly, but carefully towards them. There were only a few feet between them and the stairs, where a shaft of light was shining across the floorboards. One of them reached out to grab her, but stopped herself.

'Come closer, my child.'

Loretta peeled her eyes away from their monstrous appearance and went down the stairs. Her mother was laying on the ground across the doorway.

'Dad, what happened?'

Far in the distance she could hear sirens.

'She didn't wake up... her breathing was so soft I thought she was...'

The sirens were getting closer and closer. Her father had her mother's head in his hands, stroking her hair. He was crying. Loretta couldn't stop her own tears. She ran out into the yard and down the driveway to help navigate the ambulance into the yard. She felt her lungs hammering in and out and she knew she was on the verge of a panic attack. In the distance she could see the blue and red lights. The sun was only just breaking over the mountains and it sent a glassy, triangle of colour along the stones.

Loretta waved her hands above her head, trying desperately to get their attention. They shined their flood lights and zoomed ahead, stopping momentarily beside her.

'Where is she?' said the paramedic in the passenger seat.

'She's up there, in the doorway,' Loretta pointed.

The ambulance skidded, leaving track marks as it rocketed towards the house. Loretta ran after it. By the time she got to the front steps the paramedics had her mother on a stretcher and were lifting it up in to the rear of the van.

'I'll follow you in my car.'

Loretta jumped into the back of the ambulance.

'Mum! Mum!'

'Please, you can't come with her.'

'But... is she going to be okay?'

They were putting heart monitors on her chest and taking her blood pressure. Her skin looked silky white.

'She's gonna be okay. We gotta get her to the hospital.'

Loretta slowly stepped back and out of the ambulance. Her father came running out of the house with car keys and his shoes in his hand.

'Loretta, I'll call you when I know something.

Okay? I don't know how long we'll be. Best you stay here.'

'But Dad!'

He swung the car door open and climbed in. The ambulance backed up and spun around, heading for the open gate. Henry looked at his daughter and sped off, following the ambulance. Loretta stood in stunned silence. Her eyes tired and smudged from weeping. She watched the cars drive away and disappear into the country side.

CHAPTER TWENTY-THREE
THE WITCH IN ME

The sound of the phone ringing had woken her up. Loretta had slept on her parent's bed by the phone, waiting for her father to call. It had been hours.

'Dad?' she snapped down the line.

'Loretta. She's doing okay now. It was touch and go.'

She started to cry openly. 'Is it my fault?'

'What? No, it's not your fault. She's dehydrated and has a virus. She's been hospitalised.'

'How long will she be in for?'

'They're saying at least three days.'

'Okay,' Loretta wept. Her shaking hands could barely hold the phone to her ear.

'I'm spending the night, then I'll come back briefly tomorrow and get changed. I'll see you then okay? Are you going to be okay in the house?'

'Yes,' she meekly answered. 'I'll be okay.'

Her father said bye and then all Loretta could hear was the dial tone. She placed the receiver back on the hook and left the room. The house seemed to throb with solitude. Should could hear the window whistling through the cracks in the floorboards downstairs. The curtains moved in the draft, flapping and swaying like ghosts.

She went downstairs and into the kitchen. The pantry door was open. She stood in front of it and examined the contents, looking for something to eat. She had no idea what time it was, but she was starving. If she was going to spend the next night or two alone, she wanted to make sure her room was full of food and locked. Three jars sat nestled on the bottom shelf. She remembered seeing them in the hallway when she first arrived, and then her dad threw them out and they reappeared back in the cupboard.

She picked the first one up and held it to the light. Whatever was in it, she was definitely not eating it. It looked like a puffy, bloated onion. Her throat constricted with disgust. She tossed it in the bin and added the other two jars to it. She put the lid on the bin to stop the smell permeating around the house. She then tucked some cheese crackers under her arm, half of a bread stick, and some salami and cheese from the fridge. There was a bag of corn chips she held with her teeth and with her other hand, she took the last bottle of iced tea.

She made her way up the stairs, trying to guess what time it actually was. When she reached the second level, she glanced something out of the corner of her eye. She spun her head around to see the first door of the witch's room, open. The familiar prickles of fear shot up her legs. She looked to the window, the sun was still out. Maybe the diary was wrong? She ran to her room and dumped the food on her bed. She stood by the door and looked down the corridor, to the east wing. She ran to her side table and fetched her phone. She snatched her small jar of pens and tipped them out, filling it with all the pen lids she could find. She tucked it into her pocket and slowly, but cautiously, made her way across the landing to the other side. She stood in semi-darkness and tried to listen for footsteps or anything that would indicate the witch had gotten out.

She approached the door and tried to glance inside, but it was too dark. She opened her phone and used the torch app. The light shone onto the ground in front of her. It was caked in mud and debris from the garden. She swung her light inside the room and was instantly sickened at the sight.

The smell was rotten, and the floor was covered in old newspapers, all wet and soggy. In one corner they piled up high, like a throne, that reached the ceiling. It was tacked to the walls and across the roof. Balls of newspapers were squished against one another, forming a barrier around a small nest. Loretta found her feet moving without any real conscious thought. She stood before the nest and her eyes peeled open in horror. Small animal bones were flung across the floor and there was scat smudged into the monstrosity, against one side.

Loretta stepped back, shining her torch around the rest of the room. There was a broken table and one chair, the legs were missing, and they were propped up against the side wall. The table top was covered in scrawling's. Some of the words were legible, others were gibberish. There were symbols and sigils, circles and upside-down triangles. The smell became so over-powering that Loretta gagged. She shined the torch across the ground and behind the table, there was no key.

She decided to get out of there quickly and ran to the door. She halted violently, almost dropping her phone. The witch was standing at the door.

'Sun has gone down now, it has.'

'Get out of my way,' Loretta said aggressively.

'Just like your mother, you are. Awful. Come into a witch's room without permission. Punishment is drowning.'

Loretta placed her hand on the jar of pen lids in her pocket.

'Give me the key back.'

'It is hidden. Olympia Sparrow, our dearest sister will be unleashed tonight. The third and final door will be opened. The witching hour is approaching. Need you, we do. For feasting. Give us energy.'

Loretta took a step back. 'Why would you eat your own flesh and blood? According to you, we're related.'

The witch twitched its fingers and started to raise off the ground several inches.

'Asleep a long time, our bones are brittle. Your mother's fault, it is. She is a witch, like us, but she locks us away,'

'You were killing people... She did the right thing,'

Loretta knew she had to get past her. Being trapped in the room was dangerous.

The witch's hair lay like muddy straw over her face. Her beady canary-yellow eyes broke the veil of hair.

'Following our true purpose, we are. Witches of the Bone and Flesh. Darkness follows us. Ask your mother why she came here. She was not well. On the verge of death, she was.'

Loretta sucked in a lung full of air and bolted towards the witch. She hunkered her head down to her chest and rammed her shoulder into the witch's abdomen. The witch screamed; a guttural, bestial roar, and was knocked backwards. Loretta ran towards her room. She slipped her hand in her pocket and pulled out the jar. The witch flew towards her, gnashing its teeth onto her shoulder. Loretta screamed out in pain dropping the jar. She had only made it as far as the landing by the middle stairs. She tried to pull away, but the its teeth were dug in. She could feel it feasting on her blood. The jar by her feet was broken, but the pen lids were all still bundled together. She kicked at it with her foot. They fanned out across the open floor. She felt the teeth recede and she fell to the ground, crawling away. The witch, still hovering a foot in the air, started to count the lids. Loretta got to her feet and ran to her bedroom door. As soon as she slammed the door shut, there was a thud behind it.

'Tricks won't keep you alive, Loretta Skellington.'

'Don't call me that!' she screamed.

She ran to her pillow and dug the diary out from under it.

'There must be an answer in here somewhere to get them back in their rooms,' she said with panic in her voice. She could hear the witch gently tapping on her door with her fingernail. Every tap reverberating in her head. She flipped through the pages, reading about the secret passages under the mansion, the lengthy diatribe of the witch's circle and the hidden paths around the house, to keep out of view. Towards the end of the journal, the pages became increasingly dogeared and torn. Red blotches covered the pages and the hand writing became more and more illegible;

...I have done the most heinous of tasks. I put the witches under a sleeping spell and removed their hearts. The potion was mixed in with their night time blood feast. They drunk feverously, savouring every gulp! I knew this wouldn't kill them, as they no longer rely on their hearts to live. I placed each one in a jar and sealed it shut.

Lorretta stood up, almost dropping the journal. 'The jars,' she gasped.

Their bodies lay in a bloodied mess on the kitchen table, ribcages exposed, and their chattering teeth echoed in my ears while they were under the spell. I vomited thrice, unable to handle the smell and the task at hand. They were sewn up, with the help of my friend and colleague, then placed in a bedroom each, with newspapers and one, single, bucket of water. The doors were locked with a key obtained from the basement. The key was returned there, and hidden amongst the others, in hope that one day, if one of them ever did escape, they would be kept in a constant loop of counting the keys, instead of searching for the Skellington Key.

Loretta thumbed through the next few pages and found one of the last entries;

God forbid they escape and roam the lands, killing and maiming. If they do, we will need to get them back in their rooms and lock the doors. The inner walls have spells written in my own blood. It will keep them from scratching the walls down or kicking the door in. Although burial or drowning would be the correct method for killing them, I cannot bring myself to kill my own flesh and blood. Maybe that is the witch in me.

The heart jars are the real key. Toss them in their rooms, then smash the glass. The witch's will rush back in and try to tear open their own chests to ram the hearts back into their ribcage. This is dangerous, as it makes them extremely powerful. But if you can manage to lock the door, they will be trapped there. Although their hearts will start to beat again, they will die eventually.

Loretta closed the book and let it fall from her hands. She knew were the hearts were. All she had to do was find the key.

CHAPTER TWENTY-FOUR
BOX OF MATCHES

The phone from her parents' bedroom started to ring. Loretta shot up in bed, the journal was on her chest. She must have fallen asleep. She leapt out of bed and ran to the door, but her eyes caught something moving. She stepped back a few paces and bent down. There was someone behind the door still. She stood up and backed away. It was a trick, she thought. To get her out of her room. But what if it was her parents calling? What if her mother was gravely ill? She couldn't take the chance with the witch; it wanted to kill her.

She climbed back into bed, not knowing what time it was and shut her eyes again. Sleep came quickly, and she found herself wandering in a dreamlike state. She was outside, under the moon. She was walking along the grass. She knew it was wet, but she couldn't feel it. She looked down and she wasn't walking at all, she was floating. She didn't seem perturbed or frightened by this. Ahead of her was the labyrinth. She approached it, but an invisible gate stopped her from entering it. She tried and tried again, but it would let her get passed the hedges. She tried a different side, still with no luck. She reached into her pocket, almost instinctively, and pulled out a box of matches. She lit one and threw it at the dry kindle that made up the walls of the maze. The fire spread quickly and feverously, taking hold of the entire labyrinth in a matter of moments. The smoke was thick and black and bellowed into the night sky, momentarily covering the moon.

'One of us you are.'

'Told you, we did.'

Loretta looked behind her and could see the two witches hovering a few feet away. They both had crooked smirks across their faces. Loretta turned back to see the maze become ash and crumble before her. In the middle of the maze, on the podium, was the Skellington key. The witches had put it back.

'The key belongs here, with us.'

'So, do you, Loretta. With us.'

Loretta didn't say anything, she simply stared at the key and tried to memorise the way in. The witches had changed the direction of the maze, making it harder to get to the middle. She felt the witches behind her start to descend on her. She couldn't move or scream. On either side of her neck they plunged their teeth into her flesh. The skin tore away, and the blood gushed into their mouths, filling them and running down their necks and dripping onto the wet ground. Loretta stared at the maze, unnerved by their insatiable appetite. She felt her blood drain from her body and her legs and arms started to shiver. Her vision blurred and she felt her body starting to drift towards the ground.

She opened her eyes, she was in her bed. She ran to her desk, quickly taking notes of the layout of the maze. She ran to the bathroom and checked her neck, it was just a dream. The bites felt so real, she shivered. She slipped her hooded jacket on and slid her cold feet into her boots. She only wore her boots when she was serious about the task ahead. She wore them when she visited the smashed car at the demolition lot.

She ran down to the kitchen and searched the draws until she found a box of matches. She slid them in her pocket and went to the pantry. The jars sat at the very rear, covered in dust again. She took them out, one by one. Inside, the pickled heart floated like a bloated and mushy artichoke. She placed them on the kitchen bench and turned back to the pantry. There was a thump from upstairs and she froze with fear. The house was deadly still and the air seemed thin and cold. She waited for the sound to come again, but there was nothing but silence. She went to the knife block and took a small carving knife and slid it into her belt loop. She searched the pantry until she found an old candle and slid it in her pocket.

'Your blood is sweet, dear,' came a voice from behind her.

Loretta spun around, almost tripping on her own feet. There was no one there. She knew the witches were playing tricks on her. They must be trying to stop her from getting the key, she thought. She ran to the back door and kicked it open. Running through the grassy knoll, the air seemed arctic. Her breath flew from her mouth in great plumes. She had the jars pressed against her chest, holding them tightly. She ran to the labyrinth and halted right before the entrance. It was dark, and a thick layer of white fog lay across the ground, making it impossible to see the path.

'When we drink your blood, you will be one of us,' said the familiar voice from the inside the maze.

Loretta held up one of the jars. The stewed heart wobbled around inside.

'You attack me, and I'll destroy your heart!' she yelled as loud as she could.

Something behind her moved. She turned around to see several shadows dart across the yard. They disappeared into the darkness.

'Stab my heart, will you girl!' the witch voice echoed. 'And we'll kill your parents.'

Loretta felt her own heart sink. She didn't want to think if the witch knew where here parents were. She stepped inside the maze and began to creep along the hedgerows to the centre.

The fog felt thick against her legs. The soupy, white mist crawled up her legs if she stood still for too long. The darkness was overwhelming, and she turned her phone torch on, but the light faded out a few feet in front of her. The moon above disappeared behind thick grey clouds, she knew the witches were trying to stop her from getting the key. She tripped on something and stumbled forward. One of the jars fell from her grip and rolled along the ground. She could hear a witch moaning a few metres inside the maze. Loretta crawled on her hands and knees, using one hand to search the ground for the jar, but she couldn't see even a few inches in front of her.

Suddenly, she heard footsteps. She looked up to see a dark figure coming from the long, hedged corridor. The mist moved for it, peeling back to let her through.

'My niece the saviour of the witches. Grateful we are, but you must die!'

The witch moved with uncanny speed. Loretta leapt to her feet and back tracked, taking turn after turn without knowing where she was going. Her ribcage pounded in and out and she could feel the veins in her neck throbbing. She tripped again but found her footing. She came to a dead end and turned around, her spare hand on the knife handle.

'We can smell your fear,' one of the witches said.

'You cannot hide from us, dearie.'

Loretta had lost all bearings of where she was in the maze. She knew she would never find her way back. She had no choice. Her parents would be mad, and she would be severely punished, but she didn't care. She placed the jars on the ground and pulled the matches from her pocket. She could hear faint footsteps coming towards her. She yanked a match from the box and struck it. The blue spark hissed and went out immediately. She quickly pulled another one, looking over to the turn in the maze where the footsteps were getting closer and closer. She struck it. It flickered for a moment. Her eyes reflected the small flame. She held it against the dry hedge and it took the flame eagerly. The fire started to climb the hedge, ignited it in a brilliant inferno. The footsteps came quicker, and a figure rounded the bend and started towards her.

'Don't come any closer,' Loretta said, pulling the knife from her belt. 'Or I'll stab your heart!'

The figure halted and was suddenly viewable in the fires light.

'Casey?'

'Loretta, you gotta get out of here.'

'How did you – '

'It doesn't matter. You have to follow me.'

Loretta carefully slid her knife back into her jean's belt and picked up the jars. The fire was growing rapidly and become more intense. Casey turned and ran, her face looked panicked. Loretta followed him, trying to catch up with him, but he kept his distance. The ran along the maze as the fire jumped from one wall to the next.

'Wait,' Loretta shouted, but Casey hardly slowed. 'I can't leave, I've got to get the key.'

'Loretta,' Casey suddenly stopped as they reached a large section of the maze. It had two options, left and right. 'It's too dangerous. The witches are stronger now…we have to get out of here.'

'I have to get the key and lock them back in their rooms. They threatened to kill my parents.'

'Loretta, if they catch you they will kill you, we have to get out of the maze, now!'

She felt the warmth of the fire as the labyrinth started to become ash; it was falling down around her in big chunks of burning debris. Casey could see in her eyes that she was going to the middle of the maze, no matter what. He took a deep breath.

'Left will lead you to the middle, right will take you back out the way you came.'

Loretta felt tears well up in her eyes as she thought about her parents and what she had done. She reached out to take Casey's hand and her fingers went straight through his.

CHAPTER TWENTY-FIVE
INFERNO

He stepped back in shock.

'Loretta…'

She looked at him puzzled. She took several steps back also; her face had started to lose all its colour.

'You're…'

'Sorry, Loretta. I wanted to tell you.'

'You're a ghost.'

Casey looked crestfallen. He looked to the fire, then back at Loretta.

'I'll help you get to the middle, but we have to go quickly.'

'You're the Marsden boy that drowned in the boating accident.'

Casey nodded. 'It's been a long time since anyone could see me.'

Casey moved towards the left path and Loretta followed. They ran down the narrowing corridors, dodging the fire as it licked and spat flames onto the path. A branch fell from above and went straight through Casey. He kept running, unperturbed by the event. Loretta struggled to carry the jars, they were getting slippery and difficult to hold. Finally, they reached a larger area that lead onto the middle. Casey stopped and turned to Loretta;

'I can help you get to the middle, but I can't go into your house.'

Loretta didn't want to ask questions, but she assumed it was because the witches had done something to the house to keep spirits out. She nodded and adjusted her grip on the jars. The hearts inside felt like they were moving.

'I'll get them back in their rooms,' Loretta said. Watching as Casey ducked and weaved through the inferno. 'All I need is the key and to get out of the maze.'

Fire started to crumble the walls. The ash floated into the sky and lay on the ground, bright orange embers still burning. Casey wanted to take Loretta by her hand but couldn't. He led the way through the remaining twist and turn and both stopped suddenly. Ahead of them there were two figures floating upside down; as if they were laying on their backs. They were several feet from the ground. Their clothes were burnt, and their faces were dirty and cut. Under them was the third jar that had been dropped in the darkness. It was still intact.

'Mum! Dad!' Loretta yelped, nearly dropping the jars.

Beside them, was the podium. The Skellington Key sat in the middle, glowing in the raging fire around it.

'Loretta,' her mother said, her mouth opening and shutting, like a fish gasping for air. 'Don't come any closer... they're here!'

Loretta was astonished by her mother's voice. A dark presence suddenly enveloped the entire area and the fire instantly went out. All around her, Loretta could see large gaps in the hedgerows; she could see the gazebo and, in the distance, the surrounding acreages. Casey spun around and started to walk backwards.

Loretta turned her head to look and could see one of the witches behind them. It was Clementine Skellington.

'Smart girl, you are. Thought your bones would be in our guts by now.'

'Loretta, you gotta get out of here,' Casey said.

Clementine moved her gaze from Loretta to Casey. The witch started to cackle.

'Your bones we did eat. Nourished us for ages, they did.' Her teeth were all crooked and black. 'Boy drowned on the boat. Couldn't swim.'

'Shut up!' Casey lashed out.

'Your whole family fought to save you, but witches are stronger.'

Loretta backed up, slowly heading for the key, but never taking her eyes off the witch.

'Casey, ignore them... there are trying to frighten you. They get power from it.'

Casey had his hands in balls of fisted flesh. He released them slowly and something from his left caught his attention.

'She is free,' said the second witch, floating through the raining debris of ash and embers.

Loretta's mother closed her eyes and started to whisper words that were so soft, they sounded like mumbling. Henry was bleeding from his nose, two of the fingers on his right hand were broken.

'Agnes Skellington,' Loretta's mother, Lilith spoke, her eyes popping open.

'Our sister,' Agnes and Clementine spoke in unison.

'Tell me you didn't let Olympia Sparrow out of her cage?'

Henry looked at his wife, his mouth was opened in shock. 'Lilith?'

'Olympia is feasting and will be out soon, needs strength to walk, she does.'

'Mum?' Loretta said, running to her. The jar below them sitting idle. She managed to shove it with her foot closer to the other jars.

'Loretta, get out. These witches are very dangerous.'

'But mum, you're okay?'

'Crashed your car, we did,' Agnes grinned. Her long, matted hair covered most of her face and chest.

'You did that?' Loretta stammered, her face twisted in anger as she turned to scowl at the witch.

'Used our powers to push it forward. Get your mother here to release us.'

Both witches started to laugh. It echoed around the now dilapidated maze.

'Mum wanted to come out here to heal, not be under your spell and do your bidding!'

'Controlled her, we did.'

'Loretta,' Lilith said, her body floating limp, hovering over the podium. 'I can't remember coming out here... I don't remember being in the house.'

'Last of our energy it took,' Clementine spoke, her feet touching the ground. She bent her knees and kneeled, as if ready to launch herself forward.

'Lilith, is this true?' Henry struggled to say.

'We controlled you too, old man. You were harder, yes you were. No witch blood in you. Harder to persuade.'

From out of the darkness came a figure walking on all fours. Its arms were outstretched, like a spider. Its back legs were bent and covered in blisters and sores. It had the same mangled and dark hair, but its eyes were red like blood and most of its teeth were missing. The figure walked past its sister and sat on the ground several feet from the podium. Loretta was so close she could reach out and grab the key, but she was locked in a state of frozen shock. The witch reached into its mouth and started to pull another tooth out.

'Olympia Sparrow,' Lilith said, her fingers started to move in peculiar motions; circles and triangles.

'Sisters,' Olympia spoke. Her voice was normal and calm. 'Been a long time since we had a family reunion.' Olympia's eyes gazed over to Loretta.

The witch threw the tooth towards Loretta and it rolled and came to a holt by her feet.

'I'm putting you all back in your rooms.'

The witches laughed again.

'A new member to our circle. Daughter of a great witch. You too will be a great witch.'

'I'm not a witch!' Loretta yelled.

'Speak to things, you do. I can tell. Dreams that come true. You are half a witch, with the power of a great witch. Show you how to use it, we can. Stay here, with us.'

'Never!' Loretta launched herself on top of the jars, latching onto them with one hand and spun around, leaping toward the podium.

Agnes and Clementine screeched and leapt forward, springing from their positions behind Olympia. Lilith ended her incantation and the binding spell was broken. She fell to the ground and sprung to her feet. Her hand was still in plaster and bandages, but she stood without help.

'Loretta, run!'

Loretta snatched the key as her mother flew forward, grappling with both Agnes and Clementine. Henry screamed and battled against the spell, but he was bound in the air. Olympia waved her hand at him and he fell into a deep coma. Loretta fumbled with the jars. She slid the key in her pocket just as Olympia descended on her. Her teeth were bared, and she swiped at Loretta with her long nails. Casey ran to her, unable to help. His hands swam straight through the witch. He looked around desperately and saw an exit through the burnt hedges.

'Loretta, follow me!'

Loretta ducked and weaved away from the witch

as it snapped its teeth shut right near her shoulder. She sprinted towards Casey, only looking back momentarily to see her mother being bitten by the witches.

CHAPTER TWENTY-SIX
HEARTS AND GLASS

Either side of the hedgerow was still hot. Loretta felt the warmth on her skin. Casey was waiting on the other side, standing in the thick fog. The mansion loomed in the background. She juggled the jars and tucked one under her armpit and held onto the other two tight as she leapt through the burnt holes in the labyrinth. She ran towards the mansion.

'I can't go any closer, Loretta. You'll have to go on your own.'

'I can't go in without Mum and Dad. What if they hurt them?'

'I'll go back, I'll distract them while you…'

From behind them came the sound of hissing and dragging. Olympia had both her parents by the hair and was dragging them through the ash covered field.

'Mum! Dad!'

'Loretta! Get inside!' her mother screamed.

Loretta ran towards the rear kitchen door and fell up the crooked concrete step. The jars flew from her hands and smashed across the door way frame. The three hearts rolled to a stop on the second step – beating.

The witches screamed and held their chests. Loretta

and Casey covered their ears and turned their heads away from the witches. Loretta apprehensively picked up the hearts and ran inside the kitchen. They were slippery and mushy. Their slow beating made her feel sick to her stomach. She bolted through the kitchen and felt the strange heavy feeling that she had felt when she first arrived. She knew the witches were putting all their power into stopping her. She moved at a sluggish pace until she reached the main foyer stair case. She took one step and felt something grip her around her ankle. She looked back and could see the witch, Agnes. Its jaw had unhinged, and it was trying to clamp down on her shin bone.

'Get off me!' Loretta screeched.

She kicked furiously at the witch, clinking its jaw to one side. The witch growled like a crazed animal and lunged forward. Its teeth scraped against Loretta's skin but didn't draw blood. The witch's left hand reached up and gripped her knee cap, applying pressure with its nails. Loretta screamed, trying desperately to keep a hold of the hearts.

'Give them to me!'

Loretta started to panic. Thoughts of the car crash and the smashing of glass and the smell of burning oil and hair came back to her in floods of memories. The witch was doing something to her, she knew it. She let one heart drop from her right hand and reached into her pocket and pulled out the box of matches. She pushed the cover off with her thumb and tossed them down the stairs onto the lobby floor. The witch snarled, bearing its broken jaw and haggard teeth. It leapt off her angrily and lay before the spread of matches, picking them up one by one. Loretta snatched the heart and ran up the stairs.

Her knee cap was bleeding in five places, blood was running down her leg into her shoe. She hobbled onto the second level landing and headed down the hallway. All the doors were open. A loud thumping came from behind her. She rushed to the first door and gripped one of the hearts in her hand. Agnes was walking with an angular gait; her bones were twisted, and her jaw was hanging loose. Her eyes glowed and both of her hands were outreached, ready to strike.

Loretta threw one of the hearts in to the first room. Agnes leapt towards Loretta. She closed her eyes readied herself to be sliced open. The witch stopped, millimetres from Loretta's face and her eyes turned to watch the heart bounce and slump against the bedroom wall. She followed it inside. Loretta peeled her eyes open and slammed the door shut. She yanked the key from her pocket and locked the door.

'Mistake you have made, dearie.' The witch's voice said from behind the locked door.

Clementine flew up the stairs, her feet dangling and only inches from the ground. Her hair wavered behind her as she rushed towards Loretta.

'Lock us up again?' she wailed. 'I will take your own heart for that!'

Loretta sprinted to the next door, feeling the witch descending on her. She tossed the heart into the room and the witch followed, as if they had no control over it. She kicked the door shut with her foot and slid the Skellington key in and turned it until she heard the familiar locking sound.

Loretta held one more heart. It was the smallest of the three and was beating very faintly. She waited for the witch to come up the stairs, but there was no sound. She placed the heart on the ground and pulled the carving knife from her belt. She held it over the heart with trembling hands, then she plunged it hard into the fleshy, decaying muscle. There was a scream from outside. She could hear it across the acres of grass and the mansion walls. Within seconds she could hear Olympia screaming inside. The sound came up the stairs and Loretta readied herself. She had pulled the knife out and was ready to stab it again when the witch emerged, dragging her unconscious parents up the stairs.

'Trick the others, you did. But I am more clever. I am older and smarter.'

Olympia dropped her parents onto the ground. They hit the wood flooring hard and didn't move.

'If you have hurt them...'

'More than hurt them, I will. Kill them, if you don't give my heart back.'

It pained Loretta to see her parent's unconscious in front of her and not be able to approach them. She wanted to pull her own heart out for causing such trouble. Loretta bent down and pushed the heart a foot closer to the witch.

'Good girl, no back away.'

Loretta did as she was told. The witch floated to the ground and stepped towards the heart. She could see this witch was far more powerful than the other two. As it approached, the witch never took its eyes off her.

'You will rot in your room, just like your sisters will,' Loretta screamed and swung the knife downwards and into the heart again.

Olympia howled and threw her hands into the air, exposing her open chest cavity. It was full of maggots and worms. They dropped onto the ground and squirmed. Loretta wretched the knife up, the heart slid down the blade and she tossed it into the room. The witch rocketed towards Loretta, its mouth ready to tear her limbs apart. It's body quickly turned and flew into the room. Loretta could hear it screaming as she slammed the door shut behind her and locked it.

She ran to her parents and wrapped her arms around them. Her mother's eyes slowly opened and stared at her; her hand wrapped around her daughter and pulled her in close.

'Loretta,' she said, her words full of warmth and sincerity.

'Mum, I thought you were dead.'

'It would take more than that to kill me,' she said with a smile.

'Where they really your sisters?' Loretta asked.

'It's a long story, Loretta,' said, her breathing was laboured.

Together they helped her father up onto his back

and gently petted his hair until he woke. He couldn't remember the maze, or the witches. Together they carried him to the bedroom and put him to bed. Lilith sat on the edge of the bed and dabbed the back of her head. It was spotted with blood.

'All those years ago, and I thought they would never be released.'

'It was my fault, Mum.'

Lilith looked at her daughter. 'No. They had built up their energy for a long time and devised a plan. You weren't to know.'

Loretta hugged her mother, they both wept.

'Tomorrow we'll leave this place. We'll hide the key and make sure no one ever comes back here.'

Loretta nodded.

CHAPTER TWENTY-SEVEN
TIME WILL TELL

The next day, Loretta had packed up all her clothes and shoes into her luggage and dragged it out near the staircase. She was carefully to be quiet in case her parents were still asleep. She went back to her room and made the bed and found the diary under her pillow. She turned around and almost screamed when she saw someone standing at her doorway.

'You found my old diary,' her mother said.

'So, it is yours?'

'I wrote it so long ago, it feels likes several lifetimes have passed.'

'If you are the sister of the witches... then it would be true.'

Lilith smiled and inched away from the door.

'What are you going to do with it?'

Loretta thought for a moment. 'I'm going to put it back.'

Lilith smiled and watched as her daughter went to the third story staircase and slowly climb it. It looked different now; the sun was beating in through the window, the dust seemed to have been blown away. The floorboards sparkled, as if they had been freshly polished. She entered the side door and slid the diary back into the bookshelf. She breathed in for a moment, and slowly walked out of the room and shut the door behind her.

Downstairs, her mother and father were eating breakfast. Her father didn't seem too worried about his memory loss or why he woke up in the hallway. He was eating breakfast and smiling at his wife.

'What do you think, Loretta? Ready to finally go home?'

'As long as Mum feels okay, then yes!'

'I feel fine, I really do,' she replied. 'My arm is still a bit sore, and it hurts to talk, but other than that, I feel great.'

Henry went to the pantry and retrieved another plate and placed it between himself and his wife. He poured out the hot baked beans over some toast and put an egg on top.

'You're gonna need to eat before we head off, it's a long drive,' he said as he scoped another helping onto his plate.

After they had finished, they all helped washing up and cleaned down the kitchen, so it was spotless. Loretta wondered when the next time would be that they would come back here. She left the kitchen and found her mother staring at the stairs that lead down to the basement.

'Do you have it on you, Loretta?' she asked, without taking her eyes off the door.

Loretta slid it out of her pocket. 'Yes.' It neither gleamed nor shone. It looked dull and lifeless.

'I think we both know what we need to do with it.'

Loretta opened the door and pulled the light string. It stammered to life and lit the stairs. Together they walked down. Loretta followed her mother, who clearly knew about the hanging keys on the chains. She stopped in front of the web of old keys and stared at it.

'I haven't been down here for a long time. It's exactly how I built it.'

'You made this?' Loretta said in shock.

'Yes, to hide that key in plain sight. I couldn't get rid of it. I had to know where it was at all times.'

There was a silver hook on the ground in front of them and Loretta bend down to pick it up.

'How did the key get from here into the maze?'

Lilith looked at her daughter. 'It was me that did it.'

'You?'

'I was under Olympia's spell. When I got here, and you let Agnes and Clementine out, they fed on enough blood for her to do the spell. One night when everyone was asleep, I felt their control over my body and I remember coming down here and searching for hours until I found it. I remember breaking the spell before it was too late and taking it out to the maze and hiding it there... but they knew.'

Loretta took in a deep breath, 'They had you retrieve it.'

'They were powerful for a short time,' her mother said, taking the key and slipping the silver hook through the key hole. 'The main thing is they are back in their rooms and the key is back here, where it belongs.'

'They kept telling me I'm a witch… like you.'

Lilith handed her daughter the key and turned her back to the chains.

'Time will tell… now put the key somewhere when even I can't find it.'

Loretta walked under the hanging chains until she reached the very back. She reached up and closed her eyes and hooked it through a rusted chain link. She brought her hand down and opened her eyes; the key had disappeared into the fray of other keys. She couldn't tell one key from the next. They walked out of the basement and locked the door behind them.

Henry was dragging all the bags down the stairs and loading them into the car. Loretta helped and then felt a strange tingling on her neck. She placed her bag in the back of the car and found her parents in the house, doing some last-minute cleaning.

'I'm just need to do something before we go, I shouldn't be too long.'

Her father looked at her mother and she nodded.

Loretta went out the front door and walked around the back of the mansion. She headed in the direction of the labyrinth. It was charcoal and had collapsed on itself during the night. There wasn't much left of the maze. She continued walking until she reached the cemetery. She wandered around looking at each grave stone until she found the one she had come to see; Casey Marsden.

'I'm sorry the witches did this to you. I feel responsible.'

'It's okay,' said a voice behind her. 'You're not responsible.'

Loretta stepped around a tall headstone to see Casey standing awkwardly with his hands in his pockets.

'I wanted to come and say bye. We're leaving now and I'm not sure if we'll be back.'

Loretta felt her eyes begin to water.

'Come walk with me down to the lake.'

Loretta followed Casey out of the cemetery and down an embarkment. She had only been here once with him, a few days prior. The trees looked bigger, but the lake was still stagnant and swampy.

'The witches are locked back in their rooms. Whatever spelled bound you here should be lifted.'

'There was only one stopping me from going in the mansion. Not just me, but my family too.'

Casey looked out over the water and could see three more apparitions. They wavered in the long beams of light coming down from the canopy. Loretta guessed them to be Casey's mother and father and possibly a little sister.

'I think my family will be different now, for the better. We've been through a lot. You should go home too.'

Casey waved to his family and his mother and sister waved back. His father nodded, beaming with pride.

'I'll go with them, but we'll always be here, if you need us.'

Casey walked along the water's surface and disappeared.

Loretta waited a few moments before heading back to the mansion. When she got there, her parents were putting the last parcels of food in the back.

'Ready, Loretta?' her father said.

Loretta looked up at the old mansion, deep down, way deep down, she was going to miss it. She hoped in the back and her mother reached over and lay her hand on her thigh.

'Hope you did everything you needed to do.'

Loretta nodded. The car pulled away and travelled down the driveway and out of the Skellington Mansion gates.

EPILOGUE

'Are you ready, Loretta?' her father yelled from the kitchen.

They had been home three days. Loretta had gone back to school and was even allowed to keep her job at the cinema, but only if she worked weekends and not school nights. Her mother was in the bathroom checking her scars when her daughter walked passed.

'How do you feel about the whole thing, Loretta?' she asked.

Loretta looked at her mother's bright pink scars. They ran around her neck, behind her ear; they were over her arms and along each finger.

'I think I'm ready. It'll will be good to finally put everything behind us.'

Her mother walked out of the bathroom and gave her a massive hug. Loretta could tell she had her strength back.

'Wow, Mum.'

Together they walked downstairs and joined Henry in the car. They didn't say much on the trip over. Loretta kept catching her father looking at her in the rear vision mirror. He looked worried. When they got there, Loretta got out of the car first and went inside.

There was a rather large man behind the counter, he was covered in grease and dirt and had a long beard and wore a filthy red cap.

'Loretta Davis,' the man said, as her parents walked in behind her. 'Come to pay another instalment on the car?'

'Not this time, Joe,' she replied. Joe looked at her with vague suspicion. 'We want you to crush it.'

Joe looked at Lilith and Henry, then back at Loretta.

'Are you sure?'

'It's time.'

Joe reached below the counter and fetched some keys.

'Meet be around the back.'

Loretta led the way through the maze of wrecked cars and broken-down machinery. She knew every inch of this place and both her parents were impressed by her knowledge of the scrap yard. They stopped a few feet from the back fence. Loretta glanced over to the hole in the fence where she would climb through at night. She looked back at the car.

It's time.

Yes.

I've been waiting for this moment.

Joe drove up in a large truck and waited for Loretta to give him the go ahead. She nodded, and he picked the car up and placed it in the crushing bay. He leapt down from the truck and strolled over to the controls. Lilith was a little taken aback by seeing the car for the first time since the accident. Henry held her close.

'Do you want to do the honours?' Joe asked Loretta, pointing to a large, flashing green button.

Loretta stepped up nervously and waited a single second, then pressed it. The walls on each side of the bay started to move in. The sound of crushing metal and glass brought back bad memories. It was over in a matter of seconds. Joe opened the latch and the square wreckage just lay there. The car was now the size of a small coffee table.

'I'll leave you guys to it,' Joe said and walked off back to the front office.

Loretta and Lilith hugged and cried as they stared at the destroyed vehicle.

'Do you feel better?'

'I feel like a weight has been lifted off me,' Loretta responded.

They let a few seconds pass before they headed back out to go home.

END

ACKNOWLEDGEMENTS

This was a novella that really wanted to be written. The pieces came together quickly, and I remember telling my sister the entire story line one Christmas day. This book is dedicated to the Witches that still are active in this world today. To those of us living on the brink and under the line of sight of those that are forced to wear blinkers. There is more to this world then we realise. For my family, friends and anyone who asks me about my books. Family is more than blood.

For more information on Mitchell visit
www.ouroborusbooks.com